W9-ASY-617

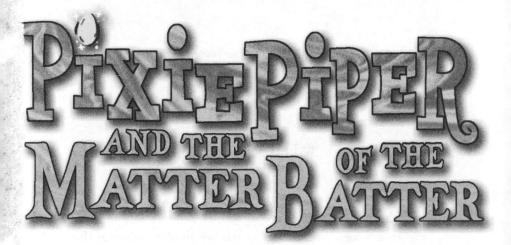

Annabelle Fisher

ILLUSTRATIONS BY
Natalie Andrewson

Greenwillow Books
An Imprint of HarperCollins Publishers

Many thanks to the bakers in Pixie's virtual test kitchen:
Stephanie Badulak
Shelley Jacobson
Melanie Lewis

Pixie Piper and the Matter of the Batter
Text copyright © 2017 by Annabelle Fisher
Illustrations copyright © 2017 by Natalie Andrewson

The text of this book is set in 11-point Arrus BT.
Book design by Paul Zakris

Library of Congress Cataloging-in-Publication Data is available.
ISBN 978-0-06-239380-7 (hardcover)
17 18 19 20 21 PC/LSCH 10 9 8 7 6 5 4 3 2 1
First Edition
 Greenwillow Books

For Zeke,
last but
not least

CHAPTER ONE
Ye olde escape

Riding shotgun in Aunt Doris's truck, with my goose,
Destiny, on my lap, I stared out the window and tried
to memorize landmarks. Woods, lakes, schools, fire-
houses—they were all starting to look alike. In the
backseat my best friend, Gray, was sitting with the
twins, River and Rain, and their goose, Drizzle. We
were on our way to Chuckling Goose Farm, but the
only one who knew what town or even what state it
was in was Aunt Doris. Unfortunately, she could keep
a secret better than a safe can keep a fortune.

Although Aunt Doris called the twins my cousins, I'd never met them before. It made us all a bit shy with each other. But Gray tried his best to be friendly by telling goose jokes.

"Why do geese fly in a vee?"

"I give up," answered River after less than a second.

"'Cause it's too hard to fly in an *s*."

"Hah!" River forced a polite laugh.

"This one's better," Gray promised. "Why do geese fly south for the winter?" He didn't even wait for the twins to answer. "Because it's too far to walk!" He cracked up. I laughed, too, so he wouldn't feel bad.

After a while Aunt Doris said, "You kids should probably try to get some sleep. We've got a long ride ahead." But there was still an hour of daylight left, and I wasn't a bit tired—until she began humming something that sounded like a lullaby. Fortunately, she still popped her gum occasionally. Aunt Doris was a real thunder-mouth, and those cracks helped me to stay awake.

I don't know how long we'd been riding when something strange happened. The truck, which Aunt Doris called Babe, was passing through filmy clouds that looked as if they'd been spun from thread as fine as spider silk. *Clouds?* I looked around and realized we were driving on a skyway rather than a highway. I glanced over at Aunt Doris. She'd put on a pair of thick goggles and was concentrating hard on the road, so I rolled down the window just enough to sneak a pinky out and snag a strand of cloud.

After that we began descending, not like a plane getting ready to land, but straight down like an elevator. As far as I could see, there was only the sea beneath us. I looked back at Gray and the twins, but they were sleeping. If I woke them, Aunt Doris would notice. For some reason it seemed important not to let her know I was up.

Just before we sank below the waves, Aunt Doris leaned over and closed my window tightly. I held my breath as the truck slipped below the surface. But when I couldn't hold it anymore, I discovered I could breathe anyway. We drove past a coral reef, where two green turtles were foraging. A school of banana-yellow fish swam alongside us for a while. But when a giant red squid tried to grab us in its tentacles, Destiny honked in alarm. Aunt Doris cracked her gum and stamped down hard on the gas pedal.

Whoosh! We shot up through the surface of the sea and rolled onto an island. My heart stopped pounding—until the ground beneath us began to quake and rumble.

Earthquake? Volcano? I wasn't sure. Then the island slapped its enormous tail.

"Hang on!" Aunt Doris whispered. I held Destiny closer as we were launched into the sky by the whale's powerful spout. We whizzed through the air until we finally landed on an icy mountain peak, sharp as the point on an icicle. Babe rocked dangerously back and forth on its tip. That was when Aunt Doris shut off the engine. "I need a nap, kiddo," she said calmly. "I suggest you take one, too."

CHAPTER TWO
Ye olde Unidentified Flying objects

"We're here," announced Aunt Doris, adding a gum crack for emphasis.

I opened my eyes and discovered we were parked in the driveway of a white farmhouse with a big front porch and a red barn beside it. A gaggle of geese honked a greeting. Destiny raised her head and fluttered her wings.

I stroked her soft back and murmured, "It's okay, those geese are going to be your friends."

"Everybody out!" Aunt Doris ordered cheerfully.

"I'll find Wyatt and ask him to help with your trunks." She headed off toward the barn.

It felt good to stand up and stretch my legs. I gazed around and saw two long picnic tables. One held platters of food. There were towering stacks of pancakes and waffles taller than me.

Two girls who'd been setting the tables dropped spoons and forks. "Hello! Welcome!" they shouted, running toward us.

For a moment I just stood there in awe. These girls were apprentices. Real, live *Goose Girls.* They were braver than brave and truer than true.

The older apprentice, a teenager with the long golden hair of a storybook princess, grinned at us. "Hi, I'm Perrin. We're really excited to have you here."

I smiled back. "Thanks, I'm Pixie."

"Oh, I know."

Hmm. I wondered what she she'd heard about me. "Do you also know Gray, Rain, and River?" I nodded toward the others.

"Now we do!" exclaimed the second apprentice. "And my name's Pip." She had sandy hair that was cropped short around her elfish ears. She looked about our age or a bit older.

"You must be starved. It's been a night and a day

since you've eaten." Perrin took me by the arm.

"But I had dinner last night—pizza. That's what we always have on Fridays," I told her.

"Last night was Saturday," Perrin said. "This is Sunday morning."

I blinked. Had I really slept for a night and a day? I caught River and Rain sending each other amazed looks.

"Well, I'm starving!" exclaimed Gray. "And the food looks awesome."

A new Goose Girl ran past the table. She was waving a butterfly net at a flock of fluttering, um, well, I wasn't sure what.

"Whoa! I've never seen butterflies like that before," said Gray.

"They're not butterflies. They're naughty biscuits!" she shouted, swinging the net. "And you're welcome to eat any you can catch."

"Oh, Nell!" Perrin shook her head. "Did you make the biscuits too light again?"

Gray's baby blues bugged out. "You mean those are flying biscuits?"

"Yes, unfortunately." Nell sighed.

"Too bad I don't have my catcher's mitt," Gray said. But he stretched up his arm like he was playing outfield and jumped. "Gotcha!" he crowed. He broke the biscuit in two and offered half to me. The salty, buttery crumbs melted on my tongue.

Rain and River began chasing the biscuits, too.

"Hello, cousins!" another voice called. With my cheeks bulging like a chipmunk's, I turned to see who'd arrived. A very tall girl was waving a net at the flying biscuits. Her thick, waist-length braid whipped across her back.

"Oh, Winnie, I added too much rising powder again," Nell told her.

"Don't worry, I'll catch them. Though it wasn't just the rising powder, you know." Winnie smiled fondly at Nell and began to chant,

"When baking biscuits rich and buttery
A heart that's light will make them fluttery
The joy that fills you helps them rise
And sends them off to sunny skies."

"It's true," Nell told us. "It happens whenever I get overexcited."

I looked around. "What were you overexcited about?"

Nell's dark eyes grew round and shiny. "Why, because you were coming, Pixie. I never met a hero before."

I felt my face grow hot. I knew my freckles were spreading from my cheeks to my ears. "I'm not a hero," I mumbled.

Perrin put a hand on my shoulder. "What you did was very brave. You eliminated our worst enemy."

"But it was an accident," I croaked. "I didn't mean to shatter her."

"Tell us how you did it," Pip pressed.

"Were you afraid?" Nell's voice quivered.

"Girls! Didn't I warn you not to bombard Pixie first thing?" scolded Aunt Doris as she returned from the barn with a long-limbed teenaged boy.

"Sorry Aunt Doris," Pip said. Nell clapped a hand over her mouth.

"Hello, new girls, I'm Wyatt," the boy said to Rain and me. Then he bumped fists with Gray and River. "It's about time we had some more guys around here. I hope you two like geese, 'cause you're going to be my assistants in the barn. We're in charge of egg production."

River and Gray both beamed.

"I thought you kids would have devoured these by now," said Aunt Doris, eyeing the waffle and pancake towers. She yawned loudly. "I'm going up to bed. Perrin, Winnie—please show Rain and Pixie the way to the kitchen when you're done eating. The rest of the Aunts are anxious to meet them."

We tucked into breakfast as though we hadn't eaten for months. Everything was as delicious as it looked. Besides pancakes, waffles, and naughty biscuits, there were bowls full of berries that glistened like jewels. The butter was creamy. The syrup shone like amber light. And no one asked me any more questions about how I'd shattered Raveneece.

While I ate, Destiny sat on my lap. I let her sip from my water glass and fed her berries from my plate. Rain and River's goose, Drizzle, walked around the table nibbling grass. But Destiny squawked when I tried to put her down, too.

"Has your goose always been shy?" asked Perrin.

"Not with my family or friends. But she's never met other geese," I replied. The thing was, Des had become clingy ever since we'd been trapped in Raveneece's hole in the woods. But I didn't want to bring that up. Talking about what had happened still gave me the creeps.

"She'll get used to the others," said Wyatt.

"I know. She just needs some time," I agreed. "I'll keep her with me till she's ready."

Wyatt sent me a sorry look. "The Aunts have a

no-geese-in-the-farmhouse policy."

"Oh." A lump rose in my throat. "Des has been sleeping with me every night since we escaped."

"Don't worry, the boy's bunkhouse is right next to the barn. Gray, River, and I will be close enough to hear her if she wakes up at night," Wyatt said.

I nodded. I could tell he'd be kind. Besides, Des loved Gray almost as much as me.

When Rain and I were so full we were holding our bellies, Perrin said, "If you're done, let's go to the kitchen so you can meet the Aunts."

Winnie nodded. "Yes, they're very anxious to meet you. But they wanted us to get acquainted first."

We slid off the bench. Wyatt stood, too, and I settled Destiny in his arms. "You're going to have fun with other geese," I told her.

But when I turned to follow Perrin, I heard Wyatt yelp.

"Yeow!"

We spun around. Wyatt was sucking on two fingers. Destiny was already fluttering at my feet.

"Oh no! Did she bite you? I'm sorry," I told him.

"It's okay," he answered. "But she sure has a strong bill."

"I know. It's what saved us." I picked up my gosling

and looked into her crystal blue eyes. "You need to go with the boys now, Dessie. I'll see you later."

"I'll take her," Gray offered.

I nodded and gave her to him. "Have fun, Des," I whispered. "Please."

CHAPTER THREE
Ye olde cone Hat

Perrin and Winnie led the way across the lawn, while Rain and I trailed behind them. Although Perrin was fair and thin, and Winnie was milk chocolatey and sturdy, their confident strides and cheerfulness made them seem very much alike. I was beginning to think I might like being a Goose Girl.

I guess Rain was thinking the same thing, because she reached for my hand. We swung them back and forth as we hurried to catch up, imitating the apprentices' wide, bouncy steps.

Suddenly Rain stopped. "Hey, where'd you get this?" she asked, fingering the fine thread around my finger.

I was surprised to see it there. "If I tell you, you'll think I'm a weirdo."

Rain sent me a sideways glance. "Maybe not."

"Well, I dreamed I was flying through a cloud and I hooked a thread of it on a finger."

"You mean it's from inside your dream?"

I shrugged. "I told you you'd think I was weird."

Rain stroked the soft, fuzzy thread that was like a ring on my pinky. "Then I'm weird, too, because I dreamed the same thing. I just wish I'd been brave enough to roll down my window."

"Thanks," I whispered. But I wasn't sure if I'd been brave—or foolish.

"Pixie! Rain! Come on!" Perrin called from the porch.

Three old women dressed in voluminous black skirts were flitting around the kitchen like giant magpies. For a moment Rain and I just stood in the doorway, watching them stirring, slicing, and rolling out dough. Clouds of steam rose from pots bubbling on the stove.

Then Winnie called, "Aunts! Pixie and Rain are here!"

"Hello and come on in, girls," said the one who'd been stirring a big pot of sauce. She wiped her hands on her ruffled apron, making her many bracelets jingle. "I'm Aunt Fancy," she said, pulling us into a hug. For an old lady, she was strong!

The Aunt who'd been cutting bread came forward with a piece for each of us. "You poor things must be hungry," she said, pressing the warm slices into our hands.

"Oh no, we're stuffed," I replied. But the bread smelled so good, I ate it anyway.

"I'm Aunt Bernie," she said when I'd swallowed the last bite. With her sleeves rolled up and her hair cut short, she seemed like the practical type. But one bite of her warm, fresh bread made me think she was an angel in disguise.

"Which one of you is Pixie?" asked the third Goose Lady. She'd been rolling out a lump of dough on the counter but stopped and came closer to inspect us.

I couldn't stop staring at her hat. It was a mountainous Mother Goose hat—cone shaped, black, and about three feet tall. I mean, who wore a traffic cone on their head when they were cooking?

Rain elbowed me.

"Er, I'm Pixie," I answered.

"You two do look alike," Aunt Fancy hurried to

say. "Same height. Same curly cinnamon red hair."

"Except that Rain's is neat," said the Aunt in the cone hat.

I looked at Rain's hair. I hadn't even realized it was cinnamon like mine. I guess it was because her hair stayed in a ponytail, even though it was curly. When I tried to wear mine that way, my curls squirmed out like worms in a downpour.

"We can't have that mop of yours around here," the old cone hat continued. "No one wants hair in their cake. You'll have to wear a hairnet if you want to work in this kitchen."

A hairnet!

"Aw, Espy, Pixie just needs a comb," said Aunt Fancy. "Girls, this is Aunt Esperanza—her name means 'hope' in Spanish."

"I brought a lot of barrettes with me. I *hope* that will help my hair." I grinned at Aunt Esperanza, *hoping* my joke would make her smile.

Aunt Esperanza stared at me. She was definitely not smiling.

I didn't get it. Old ladies usually liked me. My mom worked in a senior residence. I played cards and mahjong with the women there. They kept candies in their pockets for me.

I decided to try one more time. "Would you like to hear a rhyme about my hair?" I asked.

Aunt Esperanza raised an eyebrow. It wasn't much of an answer. But I took a deep breath and gave it a go.

"No spray or potion anywhere
Will tame my mess of crazy hair
Nor will hats or hairnets win
My hair refuses to give in
But if I got a wishing cake
Here's the wish that I would make
I'd ask for hair that's super straight
Until then, spunky hair's my fate."

Aunt Esperanza looked down and rubbed at a spot on her apron.

"Very nice, dear," Aunt Fancy said.

"It sure was," agreed Aunt Bernie. "Did you make that up just now?"

"Yes."

"Did you hear that Espy? She wrote it on the spot."

"Of course I heard. I'm not deaf," the old cone hat said.

Aunt Fancy put an arm around Rain and me. "We'll see you two later. Now go and explore the rest of the place." She lowered her voice. "And don't mind Aunt Espy."

CHAPTER FOUR
Ye olde Dormmates

Perrin, Winnie, Nell, and Pip were sitting on a bench outside the kitchen, waiting for us. "How about we show you our dorm?" suggested Perrin.

"You can unpack now if you'd like," Winnie added. "Wyatt just dropped your trunks off upstairs."

When Perrin noticed my surprised expression, she smiled. "What's wrong?"

"Nothing. It's just that my dad is like an oak tree—tall and wide—and he struggled to carry my trunk down from my room. I can't imagine Wyatt doing it. He's kind of, um, scrawny."

"Oh, he didn't do it himself," Pip said. "Perrin helped him."

Princessy Perrin? That seemed even stranger to me.

"Thanks," Rain and I said at the exact same time. It made us giggle.

We passed the second floor, which Pip explained was "the Aunts' floor." Our room, or dorm, as Perrin called it, was on the third. It had two perfectly straight rows of beds, which was probably how a bunkhouse at a summer camp looked. Since I'd never been to camp, it made me think of the dormitory room in the Madeline picture books, where twelve little girls did everything "in two straight lines." I'd always thought the best parts of those books were when Madeline didn't follow the rules.

"These two are yours," said Perrin, pointing at the two beds nearest the door. "Each summer you'll move up until, eventually, you get the beds by the window. That's where I sleep now."

"I don't mind being by the door," I said. "It will make it easier to sneak out if I need to."

"Very funny," Perrin said.

But I hadn't really been joking.

"Let's help each other unpack," Rain suggested.

"We can do your trunk first."

"Can I help, too?" asked Pip. She'd been lying on her bed on the other side of Rain's, tossing and catching a small red ball.

"Sure!" Rain and I agreed. I pulled out the top drawer of the little white chest beside my bed. Each of us had our own.

When I opened my trunk, my baby brother, Sammy, was smiling at me. The last thing I'd packed was a framed photo that had been taken when he'd turned one. He'd just eaten his first slice of cake, and there was so much frosting on his face he looked like he had a beard.

"Oh, he's so cute!" Pip exclaimed, snatching it up. "Do you have any other pictures of him?"

"Just this." I reached into a silk bag Mom had made for keeping items like barrettes and pulled out a silver chain with a locket. My parents had given it to me as a big sister gift when Sammy was born. I hadn't worn it much lately, because the chain always got twisted in my hair. But I hadn't wanted to leave it behind. "This is Sammy's first photo," I said as I opened it. "He pretty much looked like a newborn extraterrestrial."

"Aw, I'm in love," Pip cooed. I think she would

have fallen for a baby naked mole rat if I'd shown her one.

"Do you have any siblings?" I asked.

"Just Wyatt."

"He's your brother?"

"Yes, unfortunately," she said, but she couldn't help grinning.

I ran my finger around Sammy's tiny face. "You're lucky you get to have your brother here."

"Actually, we're orphans. We don't have anywhere else to go."

Even though Pip didn't sound upset, I felt as if I'd said the wrong thing. "Oh, sorry! Um, my mom was an orphan, too," I babbled. I began stuffing clothes into drawers without paying attention to what I was doing.

"It's okay. I live here all year with the Aunts. It's like having four mothers."

"That sounds fun," I said, although I wasn't so sure about Aunt Cone Hat.

I reached back into my trunk and pulled out the most important thing I'd brought from home, my quilt.

"Ooh, pretty!" Rain exclaimed.

Perrin was brushing her hair in front of the mirror,

but she stopped to see what Rain meant. "That is a beautiful quilt," she agreed. "Did someone sew it for you, Pixie?"

"Yes, my mom. She made it out of patches from her old costumes." I'd brought the quilt so I'd have a little piece of my mother with me. But as I ran my hand over a patch of green velvet, I felt homesick. I must have looked it, too, because suddenly the other girls crowded around me.

"Show us what else you brought," said Winnie. "You can tell a lot about a person by the things she chooses to pack."

"Um, okay." I plucked a tiny red cowgirl hat from my trunk. "This is Destiny's favorite hat. It's really too small for her now, but I like keeping it anyway." I set it on the chest next to Sammy's photo.

"What's this?" Pip was holding the rolled-up drawing I'd hidden at the bottom of the trunk.

"That's *personal*," I replied, but she was already smoothing it out on my bed.

"Oh, a drawing of you. I like the cinnamon-colored hair and your chocolate-sprinkle freckles." Pip studied the signature at the bottom. "Who's Leo?"

"A boy in my class." Quickly, I began rolling it up again.

"I thought Gray was your *boyfriend*," she teased.

"They're both just friends," I insisted. "Gray and I have known each other practically forever."

"Pip! Don't make her mad or—" Suddenly Nell put her hand over her own mouth. The other apprentices sent her disapproving looks.

I stared hard at all of them. "Or I might what? *Freeze someone?*"

"Pixie, no one thinks that," Perrin said. "We know you wouldn't hurt us."

Nell twisted a curl around a finger. Her chin was quivering. "I'm truly sorry," she murmured. "They call me Nervous Nellie sometimes."

I reminded myself that my power was scary, even though I wasn't. "Look, I never meant to shatter Raveneece Greed," I said, trying to explain. "But she'd trapped Destiny and me in this cave underground and she was going to keep us there until I taught her to rhyme. It was impossible! I would have been there forever."

"Holy goose!" Pip exclaimed. "How did you escape?"

"Destiny pretended to play dead. Then she surprised Raveneece by biting her nose so hard that she let go of her. I snatched Des up and began climbing a really high ladder, which was the only way out. But Raveneece grabbed the ladder and shook it so hard, I almost fell off. So I chanted a rhyme that made her stiffer than a statue and I got away. But she didn't shatter into pieces till I accidentally dropped a key on her. I didn't even know it could happen."

The apprentices were staring at me as if they'd turned into statues.

"Um, who is Raveneece Greed?" asked Rain while the others were quiet.

I took a deep breath. "A relative of ours, but not a good one. She's descended from Mother Goose's four siblings, the Sinister Sisters."

"Raveneece is horrible. She has green hair and orange teeth," squeaked Nell.

"Actually, she has orange hair and greenish teeth," I said.

"She only appears at night, like a vampire," Pip added.

I shook my head no. "Unfortunately, she can appear anytime."

Nell gasped and grabbed onto Winnie's arm.

"Like Mother Goose's greedy sisters from long ago, Raveneece wants to bake wishing cakes to sell," I added.

"But that would spoil our mission," said Rain.

I nodded. "That's why Mother Goose made a wish that took away her sister's rhyming ability *forever*! No Sinister Sister since then has been able to rhyme."

Perrin's eyes lit up. "Aha! That's why she needed you to help her rhyme."

"But you didn't do it," said Nell, "so you *are* a hero."

I shook my head. "Not really. I was desperate to get Destiny back and get away. Aunt Doris thinks the Sinister Sisters will want revenge for what I did to Raveneece."

"Do you think they'll come here?" asked Pip. She sounded excited. She still didn't understand how dangerous Raveneece was.

I shrugged. "She might. I'm really sorry."

Winnie put an arm around me. "That's okay, Pixie. If it wants to, trouble can always find its way. It doesn't need a reason. No one here is mad at you."

"Aunt Cone Hat is."

Perrin's smooth face scrunched up. "Aunt Cone Hat?"

"She means Aunt Esperanza!" said Pip. She and Nell began to giggle.

But Perrin didn't say a word or make a sound. Her

silence made them quiet down. "Aunt Espy's been on this farm forever," she explained. "She's worried that the Sinister Sisters will try to destroy it. But it's right that you should be here. You're part of our family. We've got to protect you."

I ran a hand over my favorite square of quilt, a print of the cow jumping over the moon. "That's because you have no choice," I said hoarsely.

"No!" Perrin protested. "It's because we wanted you with us from the moment Aunt Doris told us about you. You're part of the family."

I felt bad about being such a grump, but I still felt grumpy anyway. I think it was because deep down, I was afraid I wasn't good enough to be a Goose Girl.

"There's something else you should know," Winnie said. "That great big cone hat Aunt Espy wears is really precious. It belonged to Mother Goose herself! It's been passed down from descendant to descendant all these years. To be its keeper is a very great honor."

I nodded as if I understood. I really didn't, though. Not until it was too late.

CHAPTER FIVE
Ye olde Pertinacious Me

In the family photo Rain took from her trunk, her mom was holding a beagle, her dad had a parrot on his shoulder, and River was cuddling a turtle. Rain had one arm around a little gray goat while hugging Drizzle with the other. Three cats—one striped, one orange, and one black—sat at their feet.

"Wow, you live with a menagerie," I said.

She nodded. "My mom's a physician and my dad's a veterinarian. They have a clinic called United Pets and People."

Pip took the photo from her hands for a closer look. "You mean the clinic treats animals and humans?"

"That's right," Rain said proudly. "It was always my parents' dream."

While she unpacked her clothes, the apprentices began telling stories about animal emergencies—cats throwing up hairballs big enough to be in *Guinness World Records*, dogs that gobbled Thanksgiving turkeys and Halloween candy, and geese that were addicted to eating socks and tights. Pip told the story of how Aunt Esperanza's goose, La Blanca, tried to bite the mail carrier. Just before she got him, the poor guy jumped back into his truck, so instead La Blanca bit the mail truck. She actually dented it. After that the mail carrier refused to come back.

Those stories made me laugh so hard my stomach began to hurt, though a little part of me worried that La Blanca would decide to pick on Destiny.

"I have an idea, let's play speed rhyming," Pip said when the giggles ran out.

"Perfect," agreed Perrin. "Everyone come sit on my bed."

"And mine." Winnie grinned at Perrin. "We don't want your bed to collapse like it did last year."

"That was because everyone was jumping on it at once," Perrin reminded her. "Anyway, I'm almost fifteen. I'm getting too old for jumping on beds."

"Well, I'm not!" exclaimed Pip.

Winnie tickled her in the ribs. "You'll probably be jumping on beds till you're ninety."

"How do you play?" asked Rain.

"One person chooses a word to start," Pip explained. "Then we each add a rhyming word. We keep going until someone can't think of one. That person gets a point. Then we start another round. At the end of the game, the one with the most points is the loser."

"And the words get harder with each round," Perrin added. "We start with three-letter words and go on to four-, five-, and so on."

"Don't forget about the jumping part," said Pip. "When you add a word, you have to jump on the bed." Pip sprang up to demonstrate, but Winnie pulled her down.

"No jumping, only bouncing on your butt," she warned.

"Oo-kaay." Pip sighed. "Let's play already! First word is . . . *pip*."

With a lot of shouting and bouncing, we came up with twenty-four words that rhymed with *pip*. Any minute, I thought, one of the Aunts would come in and scold us. The game slowed down as we began running out of words. On my next turn, I couldn't think of anything, so I shouted, "BEAN DIP."

Perrin, Winnie, and Nell burst out laughing. But Pip said, "You're out! No two-word answers allowed."

"Oh, Pip, we never explained the rule about two-word answers. Or said that compound words are okay," said Nell. "Pixie should get a do over."

Perrin and Winnie nodded in agreement.

"Ooo-kay," Pip said. "Try again, Pixie."

But I couldn't come up with the twenty-fifth word that rhymed with *dip*. So I got a point.

"It's okay. You're just learning," Pip said a little too sweetly. "Let's try another round. The new word is . . . *push*."

"Bush!" Rain shouted so fast, she surprised me.

"Smush," Perrin added.

Nell hesitated a second. "Um, ambush."

"Gush," said Winnie next.

Perrin sent her a big, gooey smile. "You're pronouncing it wrong, cousin. It's g-uh-sh, not goosh."

"No, it's goosh. Like a peanut butter and jelly sandwich with too much filling."

Nell put a hand on each of their shoulders. "In the interest of Goose Girl unity, I think we should accept it."

Perrin nodded. Reluctantly.

It was my turn. But all the words that rhymed with *push* had been used up. Out of the corner of my eye, I saw Pip grinning again.

I flashed her a smile and bounced hard on the bed. "Platypush!" I yelled.

The Goose Girls stared at me.

"Oh, is that a cousin of the octopush?" Rain asked, making everyone, including me, laugh.

But I still got another point.

Winnie shook her head. "What Aunt Doris told us about you is true, Pixie Piper. You are pertinacious!"

I was going to have to look that one up.

CHAPTER SIX
Ye olde Dinner of Doom

At four o'clock I followed the girls downstairs for Sunday dinner. It was the same time the senior ladies at the nursing home ate, which seemed pretty weird. But Perrin explained that it was so we could be in time to watch *Good News of the Week* on TV. No one wanted to miss it.

"I don't think we have that show at home," I said.

"Oh, it's our favorite around here." Perrin smiled mysteriously. "You'll see why."

The dining room felt like a museum. The walls

were covered with framed pictures of birthday cakes. There was one that reminded me of a photo I'd seen of a skyscraper disappearing into the clouds. It had so many layers they didn't all make it into the picture. Another frame held a picture of a strawberry shortcake that looked like a royal crown, frosted in whipped cream swirls with pointy tips that were studded with jewel-like berries. But the one that held my gaze the longest was a simple, round cake—the two-layer kind—with frosting that wasn't snow white but more the delicate color of old lace. The only decoration on top was an X formed by two reddish brown cinnamon sticks. I could practically smell its sweet, nutty scent wafting right out of the picture.

We were just sitting down on a bench at the long oak table when the boys came in and sat across from us. Gray looked happy. Before I could ask him how Destiny was, the Goose Ladies—or Aunts, as they called themselves—came in carrying bowls and platters. After they'd arranged them on the table, Aunt Doris, Aunt Fancy, and Aunt Bernie settled on the same side as the boys. Aunt Esperanza sat in a high-backed chair at the head of the table. She was still wearing the traffic cone on her head. I gazed at the big bowls of spaghetti, sauce, and cheese. Everything smelled delicious, and I couldn't wait to dig in. We'd just begun serving ourselves when Pip exclaimed, "What happened to your nose, Wyatt?"

"Just a little bite," he answered, lifting a hand to the bandage over the top of his nose.

"Really? Which goose?" asked Aunt Esperanza.

I put down my fork. I was pretty sure I knew the answer.

Wyatt hesitated as if he were reluctant to say. "Destiny," he admitted finally. "At first, when we brought her into the barn, we put her down with the others. But she raced for the door." Wyatt shrugged. "I wasn't expecting her to try to escape, but she's new. When I caught her, she nipped my nose. It's my fault. I should have been more careful."

"I'm sorry," I said. "I think she's scared here."

"She'll fit in," said Wyatt. "It will probably take her a while to get comfortable. She's a runt, you know. The others are all bigger than her."

A lump formed in my throat. I hadn't realized Des was a runt.

"She's going to have to fit in soon or we'll have to cage her," said Aunt Cone Hat. She turned toward me. "It would be for her own good. It's dangerous for a little goose to wander around alone."

Gray and I exchanged wide-eyed looks across the table. "I'll make sure it doesn't happen again," he promised.

Aunt Cone Hat looked at him. "We'll see," she muttered.

For a moment it was dead quiet. Then Aunt Bernie said, "If we don't start eating, everything will get cold. Somebody pass the pasta."

"Did you know that Wyatt made the cheese with milk from our cows, Ivy and Fern?" Winnie asked Rain and me.

Nell giggled. "Yes, those two are in love with him. Truly! They kick anyone else who tries to milk them."

"So Gray and River, you'd better be careful when you're cleaning up the cow patties," said Wyatt.

Gray laughed. He didn't mind being teased. It was a good thing, too, because there was a lot of it going on. Wyatt was the girls' favorite target. They stole the bread off his plate when he wasn't looking and passed him the pepper when he asked for salt. He pretended not to notice, but I think he enjoyed their pranks.

The Aunts hardly said a word, though occasionally they'd catch my eye and smile. Except for Aunt

Esperanza. The looks she sent me were scary. *She* was scary. Her eyes were shriveled like old raisins, her wrinkles had wrinkles, and her chin was round like a light bulb. And of course, there was that hat. I wondered if it was glued to her head.

Perrin clinked a spoon again her glass. "Let's hurry and clean up. It's almost time for *Good News*."

I cleared my place and started to follow the girls to the kitchen.

"Just a minute, Pixie," said Aunt Cone Hat. "We want to speak to you."

CHAPTER SEVEN
Ye olde Bad Talent

I sat back down, wondering how I could be in trouble already and watched as Aunt Esperanza retied her hat. With her gnarled old fingers, it took a while, and her face scrunched up as if it hurt. I felt kind of sorry for her.

"We're glad you're here, Pixie," she said finally. "Doris has told us all about you. With your help, we're hoping to bake more cakes with even stronger wishing powers."

I sat up taller. Maybe I wasn't in trouble. I

wondered if I might get to wear a tall black hat some-day. Then I started imagining how Destiny would look in a goose-sized version.

Crack!! Aunt Doris snapped her chewing gum. The expression on her face warned me to pay attention.

"However, in spite of your power, I don't know if you'll pass your apprenticeship," Aunt Esperanza continued. "Because you'd have to follow the rules. And so far, you've been failing at that."

"But I've been braver than brave and truer than true!" I looked at Aunt Doris. The smile she sent me was small and cautious.

"You were disobedient. You didn't listen to Doris when she told you to stay away from Raveneece," Aunt Bernie said.

It was true, but it felt unfair.

Aunt Fancy's bracelets jingled as she reached across the table and patted my hand. "It's how you got in so much trouble, dear. We're just trying to keep it from happening again. The next time you might not be so lucky." She bit her lip, looking worried.

"But I was supposed to guard my goose. That was a rule, too. You're not being f—"

Old Cone Hat's glare stopped me from finish-ing my sentence. "You have to be able to recognize what's most important," she said. "And you've got to use self-restraint. Though so far, I'm not convinced you have any in you."

"Come on, Espy," Aunt Doris said. "Pixie didn't know how dangerous Raveneece was. And she had no idea about the strength of her own power."

Aunt Cone Hat rapped the table with her knotty knuckles. "She didn't just break a rule, Doris! *She shattered Raveneece.* The Sinister Sisters are bent on revenge. Every person and goose on this farm is now threatened."

"I didn't do it on purpose," I said. "I didn't even know it could happen."

"That doesn't matter to the Sinister Sisters," Aunt Esperanza snapped. "You've got a talent for trouble—and trouble is exactly what we *don't* need here. You are not to set foot off this farm. And you're never to be alone. Understood?"

I stared at her with my mouth wide open. She was being so mean! A rhyme popped into my head:

"Underneath that pointy hat

Is your head pointy, too?

I'm not the one who doesn't get it,

Aunt Cone Hat, it's you!"

Okay, I didn't actually say it. None of the other

Aunts spoke, either. I glanced at Aunt Doris, but she wouldn't look at me.

"Yes, understood." I sighed.

"Now go and join the others in the TV room." Aunt Esperanza dismissed me with a wave like she was shooing a fly.

"Okay—but can I go to the barn to check on Destiny for a couple of minutes first? I haven't seen her since this morning."

"No! That goose needs to learn to be without you. And the sooner, the better!"

CHAPTER EIGHT
Ye olde Good News

In the TV room, I joined Gray, Rain, and River on a rug that was as soft as the fur of a Persian cat. We were closest to the TV and farthest from the Aunts, who sat in wooden rocking chairs at the back of the room. Right behind us, Perrin, Nell, Winnie, and Pip were settled on a cherry-red sofa. Winnie leaned forward and patted me hello when I sat down.

"What did the Aunts want?" whispered Gray.

I scooted closer and murmured, "They think I've got a talent for trouble."

He rolled his eyes. "Everyone already knows that, Pix. So what?"

"So I'm supposed to follow the rules, no matter what."

"Turn it on, Wyatt, or we'll miss the beginning!" commanded Aunt Esperanza.

Wyatt had been leaning against the doorframe, munching popcorn. But at Aunt Esperanza's command, he snatched up the remote and clicked it at the TV screen.

The show opened with music that sounded like chirping and a line of cartoon birds on a telephone wire tweeting to one another. Then a real live woman with spiky blond hair looked up from some papers on her desk and said, "Happy Friday! I'm Toni Tellsit, and this week we're highlighting two Good News stories."

"Ooh, I like Toni's outfit tonight," said Aunt Fancy. "That yellow dress is very becoming."

"Fancy, you like anything with a bow," chided Aunt Bernie. "The one she's wearing is big enough to decorate a dinosaur in an Easter parade."

"Quiet, you two!" Aunt Cone Hat snapped.

"The first story tonight is about the opening of a new playground at the children's hospital in

Rainbow Ridge," Toni Tellsit began. "It's designed to be friendly to kids with disabilities, as well as those who can get around under their own steam. But before we take you there, we want to introduce you to the young men who helped make it happen, eight-year-old Corey Robin and seven-year-old Robbie Robin."

The camera focused on two boys with eyes as big as quarters and mops of dark hair. They looked alike, although there was one big difference. Robbie was in a wheelchair.

"Okay, boys, tell us how you did it," said Toni.

Corey shrugged. "Well, before, when I went to the playground, Robbie always came along to watch. I wanted a place where he could do stuff with me."

"And how did you put your idea into action?"

Corey pushed his hair out of his eyes. "I made a wish on my birthday cake."

Perrin, Nell, Winnie, and Pip clapped.

"Shh!" the Aunts chorused.

"And what happened next?" asked Toni.

"It was weird. The week after my birthday, this lady who's a playground engineer, Ms. Handly, knocked on our door," Corey explained. "She said Rainbow Ridge Hospital had asked her to build a playground for them. They told her to talk to Robbie and me about it, because Robbie's spent a lot of time there."

Toni grinned at him. "I heard that you helped with the fund-raising, too,"

"A bunch of us kids did," Corey said. "We held car washes, did yard work, walked dogs, watered plants, and ran errands."

"I sold lemonade," Robbie added.

"Let's show our viewers the results of all that work," said Toni. "Here's a videotape."

The new Rainbow Ridge Playground was bustling with children playing on a pretend pirate ship. There were lots of ramps and wide doors for kids who were in wheelchairs or who had trouble walking up stairs. There was also a push carousel that had spaces for wheelchairs and a row of swings that alternated high-backed ones with the usual backless kind, so that kids like Corey and Robbie could swing next to each other.

The idea that it might have been one of the Goose Ladies' cakes that made Corey's wish come true was super amazing.

After a commercial, Toni reappeared on the screen with a shaggy-haired man in a Beatles T-shirt. "Next, meet Mr. Melvy Moonpie," she said. "For seven years Mr. Moonpie has been collecting pickles that look like the members of his all-time favorite band, the Beatles. And the good news is, this week he finally completed his collection. Please tell us your story, Mr. Moonpie."

"Well, Toni, when I was young, I began collecting anything that had the Beatles' names or faces on it—posters, T-shirts, mugs, shoelaces, slippers, towels, hats, scarves—everything right down to my boxers."

"Er, about the pickles," Toni reminded him.

"Well, one day, I was having a ham and cheese at Pete's Diner. I always order a whole pickle on the side, because Pete's are the crunchiest. Anyway, I was about to bite into a mean, green one when suddenly I was face-to-face with Paul McCartney!"

"Your pickle looked like Paul McCartney?"

"Yep."

"That must have been amazing!" exclaimed Toni.

"I think this nut's cracked," muttered Aunt Bernie.

Gray rolled off his cushion, snickering. Rain and I elbowed each other in the ribs.

"Yep! That pickle had the face of Paul, there was no mistaking it," Melvy Moonpie continued. "But to make sure I wasn't dreaming, I showed it to the waitress, Minnie Crackers."

"And she cracked up," Gray whispered. He and River both buried their faces in their knees.

"And what did Minnie say?" asked Toni.

"She shouted so loud it set the neighborhood dogs howling. *'Congratulations, Melvy, you've finally found Paul!'"*

I looked over at Gray. I was afraid he might die laughing.

"Was Paul more difficult to find than the other three pickles, I mean, Beatles?" Toni asked.

Melvy rubbed his chin. "John was easiest—he came with a corned beef sandwich. George was in a dish with pickled tomatoes and peppers, but I had to stop my nephew from biting into him. Ringo was in a jar I found at the back of my sister's refrigerator. Lucky for me, she never throws anything out. But it took me seven years to find Paul. I'd wished for him on my birthday cake the night before, and there he was!"

"Viewers at home, you are in for a treat," Toni said. "Melvy Moonpie has brought his collection of pickled Beatles into the studio today. Here they are."

Melvy stood behind a table that held four medium-sized glass jars. Slowly, the camera focused on each one. The water the Beatles floated in was pretty murky. They were wrinkled, bumpy, and old. They looked like *pickles.*

"If you ask me, those things are stomachaches waiting to happen," grumbled Aunt Cone Hat.

"So I guess finding Paul was the best day of your life," said Toni.

Melvy turned a crooked-toothed smile to the camera. "Oh no. The best day of my life was selling my pickle collection to another Beatles fan. He'll be picking them up right after this show."

Toni's eyes widened. "After all the trouble you went to?"

"It's time for someone else to enjoy them," Melvy said. "You see, ever since I read about the oil spill in Alaska, I've wanted to go there to help clean up the shores and restore the area for wildlife. But until now, I couldn't afford the airfare. It's been my wish for a long time, and now I'm finally off to Fairbanks next week!"

CHAPTER NINE
Ye olde Night of Secrets

I'd been thinking we'd have some free time when *Good News of the Week* was over. But Aunt Esperanza said, "Good night, apprentices." She made it sound like it was an order.

I turned to Gray and rolled my eyes. He sent me back a burp and followed River and Wyatt. The three of them were sharing a room right near the barn. According to Wyatt, it was so close they could roll out of bed to milk Ivy and Fern.

"Good night, Aunts," Perrin chirped, speaking for

all of us. She headed upstairs with Nell, Winnie, and Pip. Rain and I followed, taking our time. We made up a game of hopping up three steps and then jumping back two, so it would take us extra-long to get to our room.

By the time I'd reached it, I had a plan. Quickly I grabbed my nightgown and toothbrush and headed for the door.

"Pixie, there are two bathrooms down the hallway," Perrin called. "And if you want to send an e-mail home, the computer room is next door. It's about the size of a closet, so don't miss it."

"Thanks," I replied, even though I wasn't ready to send my family the cheerful note I knew they were hoping for. But the door to the computer room was open. The room was tiny, but cozy and inviting. The walls were papered with a print of geese wearing tutus, and a small wooden table with a computer was waiting like an invitation. It seemed so cozy and private that I plopped right down.

TO: Lucy Chang, Alexa Pinkston
SUBJECT: My First Day
This baking camp is for the birds
The staff is strict, the kids are nerds

The place has more rules than a jail
I think at camping, I might fail
The only thing that's good's the cake
I think I made a big mistake

Miss you!
Pixie

After I clicked Send, I continued on to the bathroom. At home I lived in the caretaker's cottage on an estate that included a museum of rare and historical toilets. I was hoping the commodes here would be shaped like geese or that they recited rhymes when you flushed, so I could tell Uncle Bottoms, who owned the estate. Unfortunately, these toilets were totally uninteresting.

I turned on the shower, but I didn't get in. Leaving my clothes and sneakers behind a stack of towels on a shelf, I put on my nightgown and slung my little goose flashlight, which I'd put on a lanyard, around my neck. Quickly, I padded back into the corridor again. I wanted the other girls to think I was in there, while I went to the barn to see Destiny. But if one of the Aunts caught me, I was planning to say I was on my way to the kitchen hoping to find a bedtime snack. I knew it was deceitful. And I felt bad about wasting water. But as Aunt Cone Hat herself said, I had to recognize what was most important. Right now, Des was at the top of my list.

"Ahem." I was heading for the staircase when someone coughed softly.

I was not braver than brave. I jumped before I realized it was Rain. "What are you doing here?" I asked.

She held up her toothbrush as an answer. "What about you?"

I decided to trust her. "I'm going to see Destiny. I'm worried she thinks I abandoned her. Don't tell anyone."

"I'll come, too. I want to see Drizzle." Rain crossed her arms over her chest as if she wasn't budging.

"We'll probably get in trouble," I told her.

"If you go down that staircase, you'll *definitely* get in trouble." I spun around at the sound of another voice. Somehow, Pip had snuck up on us.

I was more disappointed than surprised. I'd thought maybe she was different from the others— less interested in following rules. "You were spying on me," I grumbled.

"Not spying—protecting. You know we're not supposed to leave you alone."

"I'm still going. I don't care if I get caught."

"Me, either," Rain added, lacing her fingers through mine.

Pip sighed. "Then I guess I'll have to break the rules and go, too. But the Aunts' rooms are right below ours and they might hear us. I'll show you a better way."

"Okay," I agreed. "Just let me turn off the shower."

We made our way to the other end of the hall, where Pip opened a deep closet with shelves packed with bed linens and towels. There was also a tall, built-in cupboard, with doors like a china cabinet. Pip swung them open. Inside was a staircase.

"This leads directly to the barn," she said. "The stairs are creaky, but the Aunts sleep pretty soundly."

"I never worry about making noise," Rain said.

"Why, are you a cat?" I teased.

She grinned. "It's my special gift—I can make myself and everything around me silent."

Hmm. Although the apprentices all knew about my ability—which I wouldn't have called a "gift"—it was the first time I'd heard anyone mention theirs. "What if you drop something?" I asked.

"It doesn't make any noise, unless I want it to."

Rain wasn't bragging; she was just stating a fact.

Pip removed one of her slippers and dangled it between two fingers. "What if *someone else* drops something?"

Rain shrugged. "Try it."

As Pip let go, Rain whispered a chant:

"Bumps and thumps, let silence fall

Stop the noises in this hall!"

She really was a person of few words. She didn't utter a single unnecessary noun, verb, adjective, or adverb.

"How did you discover it?" I asked.

"Our house is next door to United Pets and People. At night sometimes, River and I sneak over and visit the animals. I discovered I could stop noise when we went to see a lonely beagle that began howling the moment it saw us and a rhyme popped out of me:

'Silence every doggie sound

While we're cheering up this hound.'"

"Wow! That's a really useful ability to have when you're living with animals," I said.

Rain grinned. "Or parents."

Pip sighed. "I'd love to see your clinic sometime. But right now we'd better quit talking and keep walking if we want to get to the barn before morning."

The staircase wound around and around in tight, sharp turns. I was dizzy by the time we reached the door at the bottom. I reached for the knob.

"Wait, it's locked," said Pip. She rubbed her hands together and began chanting.

"Door, door, please let us in

To greet whatever lies within

I have no key, nor can I knock

So with this rhyme, release your lock!"

Click! The lock turned and I yanked the door open. I couldn't wait another minute to see my goose.

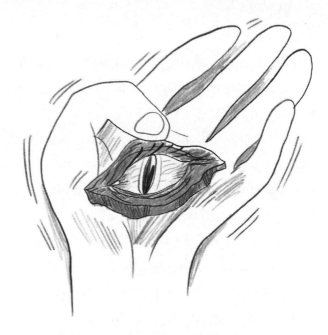

CHAPTER TEN
Ye olde Evil Eye

The moon that shone through the high, round barn window cast a glow over a gaggle of sleeping geese. With their heads resting on their backs and their beaks tucked under their wings, they looked like a flock of pillows. But when they heard us, some of them began to awaken. Two rose and waddled over.

"That's my goose, Bubbles, but I call her Bubba," said Pip.

I could see why. Bubba was the size of a king-sized pillow.

"Hi, sleepy," Rain said, lifting Drizzle in her arms. She turned to Pip. "It looks like our geese are friends."

I felt a quick flickering in my throat. I'd expected Destiny to come walk-running to me, flapping the way she did whenever she was in a big hurry. But I didn't see her anywhere.

"Destiny! Des!" I called. When she didn't appear, my knees became shaky.

"Look again. She's probably in the goose pile. They all look pretty much alike when they're sleeping," Pip said.

"No—you don't know her. She doesn't like for us to be apart. She would've come right away." My skin was damp, my heart thumped, and my voice was panicky to my ears. Some of the other birds began to stir.

"Oh, Pixie, we'll find her," said Rain, taking my arm.

"Yeah, there are a lot of hiding places in here," Pip agreed. "She's probably just tucked herself into a corner."

"But why wouldn't she sleep with the others?" I asked.

Pip shrugged. "Bubba and I will climb up and

check the hayloft." Tucking the chubby goose under her arm, Pip began making her way up the loft ladder. Watching her made me shudder. The last time I'd climbed a ladder, I'd been escaping from Raveneece Greed.

The barn was full of strangely shaped shadows. But I made myself ignore them. I began searching behind bales of hay, wheelbarrows, sacks of feed, and other stuff. I also checked the stalls where the cows, Ivy and Fern, and the old farm horse, Thomas, were resting.

Thomas nickered a greeting as I climbed on the gate to look in his stall. He seemed so sweet and gentle, I thought he'd be a good companion for Destiny. But she wasn't in there with him, either.

"Where is she, Thomas?" I murmured. "Don't the other geese like her?" I hadn't forgotten what Wyatt had said about Des being a runt. It hurt to think that maybe the bigger geese had been ignoring her, or worse, that they'd been picking on her.

Aunt Doris had said Chuckling Goose Farm would be a safer place for us. But even here, I never should have left Destiny alone. I was worried that she'd escaped, that she was wandering around in the dark, looking for me.

"Destiny! Destiny!" I yelled. I no longer cared who heard me. But I upset the geese. It seemed as if they all began honking at the exact same time. The barn sounded like a traffic jam.

Quickly, Rain climbed atop a bale of hay and yelled:

"In this barn that's filled with geese
All the honking now must cease!"

Just as the geese stopped honking—*bam!* A door toward the back of the barn flew open and crashed against the wall. In rushed Wyatt with Gray and River right behind him. Gray was carrying Destiny.

When she saw me, Des flapped out of Gray's arms and into mine. She was shaking and making a nervous muttering sound.

"I thought she was gone!" I cried.

"Sorry, Pix," said Gray. "I heard her honking, so I decided to let her sleep with me."

Wyatt reached over and stroked Destiny's head. "I'll bet you spoiled her at home."

"She's not spoiled," I sniffled into her feathers. "She's been sleeping with me every night since we escaped from Raveneece, but it was for *me*, not for her. I've never seen her this upset. She must have heard something outside. An animal or—"

Gray and I locked eyes. I knew we were both thinking the same thing.

"Okay, we'd better check." Wyatt pointed his big flashlight at River and Pip. "You two go out and check the little barn. Make sure the eggs and the hatchlings are okay. Gray, you get the geese settled down here. Pixie and Rain, you come with me."

"Stay here, Destiny," I said, handing her to Gray. I was relieved when she snuggled into his arms.

Wyatt lifted the heavy latch on the barn door and opened it just enough for us to get out. The cool night breeze ruffled the bottom of my nightgown and the grass under my feet felt damp. The moon was bright, but I turned on the little goose flashlight and aimed it at the grass.

"You and Rain start on that end," Wyatt said, pointing his light to the right, "and I'll start on the other end."

"What should we look for?" asked Rain.

"Animal tracks, feathers, or tufts of fur. I guess there could have been a fox or an owl out here," said Wyatt. He hesitated a moment before he added, "Or human footprints."

Rain and I walked silently with our heads down, searching every inch of ground. But I stepped on something sharp anyway. It stuck in my toe like a big splinter.

"Ow!" I yelped, plopping down in the grass. I pulled it out and stared—*and it stared back!* It felt like a piece of broken pottery—sharp and jagged—but it was an eye. Carefully, I closed my fingers over it.

Rain dropped to her knees. "What happened?"

I put a finger to my lips and opened my fist. "Can you hold this for me—*please?*" I begged Rain. "I'll explain when we're alone."

"Sure."

I dropped the eye into her hand just before Wyatt reached us. "Are you okay?" he asked.

My stomach felt like it had just gone for a spin in the clothes dryer. But I said, "Yes. I must have stepped on a sharp pebble or a stick. It's only a little cut."

Wyatt crouched down and looked at my bloody toe. For a moment I thought I was going to get a scolding. But he only said, "It doesn't look too bad. Come on. I'll give you a piggyback inside and fix you up with the first-aid kit."

CHAPTER ELEVEN
Ye olde Watchgoose

Rain and I dawdled getting ready the next morning. "How's your toe?" she asked when the rest of the apprentices left for breakfast.

I wriggled it. "It doesn't hurt much. Can I have the, um, splinter back now?"

She dug it out from under her mattress. "Is it really an eye, Pixie?" she whispered.

"Yes, it belongs to Raveneece Greed." Just saying her name sent a shiver down my back. "At least, I'm pretty sure it does. The last time I saw it was after I'd shattered her."

"How do you think it got here?" We both looked around as if Raveneece were watching us.

"That's what I need to find out."

"Are you going to tell the Aunts about it?"

It was a question I'd been asking myself. If Raveneece or her sisters had been sneaking around Chuckling Goose Farm, it meant danger was just over our shoulders. But if I did tell, Old Cone Hat might send me home—and the trouble would surely follow me there. I didn't want *them* anywhere near my family. My little brother, Sammy, would be as easy to snatch up as a newly hatched gosling.

I swallowed hard before I answered, "I'll tell Aunt Doris—soon. But I'm going to keep it a secret a little longer. Okay?"

"Sure," Rain agreed.

I opened the bottom drawer where I kept my socks and pushed the eye inside a balled-up pair of blue-striped ones. "Thanks for keeping it for me last night," I said. "You were kind of like the girl in 'The Princess and the Pea.'"

Rain grinned. "I liked knowing it was under the mattress."

"You're weird," I said. Then I gave her a hug.

* * *

At breakfast Aunt Cone Hat sat across the table from me. Maybe it was just my own guilty feeling, but every time I looked up, she seemed to be staring at me. The pancakes were fluffy and the berries were big and juicy. But I was having trouble eating anything. I was afraid Wyatt might tell her about the commotion Destiny had caused in the barn.

"We're having a wishing rhyme session after breakfast this morning," Perrin announced. She looked at Rain and me. "Don't forget your poetry notebooks."

"Are we going to bake, too?" I asked.

"You can't bake without the right rhyme," she replied. Her closed-mouth smile made me curious.

Suddenly there was the sound of a *honnnk!* close by. Most people think that a honk is a honk, but they're wrong. There are differences from goose to goose. And I *knew* what all of Destiny's honks sounded like. This one meant she was looking for me.

I jumped as if I'd just sat on a cactus. "May I be excused? Please!"

But it was too late. Des came goose-trotting into the dining room. When she saw me, she let out a big, joyful *HONK!* and hurried toward me.

Aunt Esperanza's face got so red I thought her

hat might shoot off her head like a rocket. "Get that goose out of—"

I scooped up Destiny and ran before old Cone Hat could finish. I didn't stop until we were in the grassy meadow beyond the yard.

"Oh, Des, I thought you'd like being with other geese," I said, plopping down with her. "I can't be with you all the time. You need to make at least one friend."

Des tugged at my hair, which she knew would make me laugh. She could always tell when I was upset.

"All right, go and graze," I told her. "At least one of us should eat breakfast."

When I looked up, I saw Gray jogging toward us. At the sight of him, I nearly burst into tears.

"I brought provisions," he said, sitting down beside me. He handed over a muffin and unfolded a napkin full of berries.

"I don't even know how Des got into the house," I said miserably. "If that old Cone Hat tries to put her in a cage, I'll go home!"

"It's okay," he said, offering Destiny a raspberry. "After you left, Aunt Doris told old Aunt Bossy Pants that she needed to give Destiny more time."

"In front of everyone?" I asked.

"Yup. And I promised to watch Des more closely, so she doesn't escape." Gray let out a burp of satisfaction.

"Thanks," I sniffled. "Do the other geese really pick on her?"

"Let's just say she's pretty low in the pecking order." Gray fed Des a muffin crumb. "You need to work on your social skills, you gooseberry," he told her.

Des touched her bill to his knee in a goose kiss.

"I have something to tell you about last night," I said. "When Rain and I were outside with Wyatt, I found something."

"You did? Wyatt didn't mention it."

"He doesn't know. I only showed it to Rain."

"What was it?"

I took a deep breath before I answered. "Raveneece's eye. At first, I thought it was just a splinter because it's hard and sharp."

"Wow!"

"I think it's the reason Des was so upset last night—and why she came looking for me this morning. She knew Raveneece was around! She's trying to protect me."

Gray let out a low whistle. "Instead of a watchdog, you've got a watchgoose." He was trying to make me smile, but I wasn't in the mood.

"You'll keep it a secret, won't you?" I asked.

"Yeah." He nodded. "But Pix, I think you should tell Aunt Doris or someone."

I couldn't help remembering what old Cone Hat had said. She was right, I did have a talent for trouble. I sighed loudly, though it came out more like a growl.

"C'mon Pix, don't be mad," said Gray.

"I'm only mad at myself," I answered. "I'll talk to Aunt Doris later. I've got to go to the rhyming session now."

CHAPTER TWELVE
Ye olde Rhyming Secret

There was a room just for writing wishing poems! It was next to the kitchen, but until now, the heavy oak door had been shut. Carved into the dark, polished wood was a poem:

> Enter, poets, if you're willing
> To create the sweetest filling
> Words that make a cake so light
> They send hope on its precious flight.

Beneath the verse was a carving of a bee hovering over a flower. I actually had a buzzy feeling as I turned the doorknob and entered.

One wall of the wishing room had tall open windows that let the morning sun stream in. I gazed out at a flower garden bursting with bright yellow sunflowers, the pinkest-pink echinacea, and a tall stand of purple verbena. The sounds of birds and the gentle breeze outside were almost like music.

I could see why this was where the apprentices wrote poetry. But my verses weren't usually the sunshine and flowers sort. Two of my best rhymes were about a four-hundred-year-old toilet and burping. I wondered what kind of poems the other apprentices wrote. I hoped mine would be okay.

"Hurry up and have a seat, Pixie. We're ready to begin," said Perrin, sounding like a teacher. She was standing at the front of the room. The rest of the apprentices were sitting or lying on big square floor pillows in rainbow colors.

Rain pointed to the green cushion she'd placed next to her blue one. I sent her a grateful smile and hurried over.

"This is the most important part of the process," explained Perrin, looking at the two of us. "You can't bake a wishing cake without a wishing rhyme. Just remember, with perspiration comes inspiration."

If Gray were here, he would have said, "With perspiration comes odor." But he wasn't. So I kept the
joke to myself and tried to look serious.

"Are there rules about writing a wishing cake
rhyme?" asked Rain.

Perrin sent her an encouraging smile that reminded
me of my fifth grade teacher, Ms. Tomassini. Out of
all my teachers, she'd been my favorite. "Just remember to use the words *wish* and *hope* at least once in
your verse or it won't work," Perrin answered. "And
don't worry! I promise, by tomorrow you'll feel like
an old hand."

"You mean we're going to write more poems
tomorrow?" I asked.

"Yes, we write every morning after breakfast,
except for delivery days and weekends."

I thought about it for a moment. "Couldn't we just
use the same rhyme over again?"

"Oh no." Perrin's eyes became big and serious.
"If you recite the same rhyme for each cake, it
gets boring. You stop listening to the words. You
stop feeling and believing them. And when that
happens, a cake's wishing power becomes weaker.
New rhymes keep your mind and heart lively."
She looked at the grandfather clock in the corner.

"We'd better get started."

The apprentices all opened their notebooks. Even Rain seemed inspired. I fidgeted with my pencil until it slipped from my hand, landed on its eraser, bounced in the air, and dropped into Perrin's lap. As she handed it back to me, I realized she was capable of frowning.

It was the same problem I had in school: I couldn't write on command. At home I was always writing, but the poems found me. To settle down, I tried counting my eyelashes by feeling them with my fingers. But I kept losing my place and starting over, until I finally ended up poking myself in the eye. That gave me the idea to close both eyes and imagine that I was at home under my favorite tree with my notebook on my lap. The beginning of a poem finally drifted into my mind.

> You cannot drink an ocean
> Or make mountains out of sand
> But any type of wish you make
> Will fit inside your hand
>
> Then hope like wind will sweep it up
> And blow it all about
> Till it lands upon a candle
> And someone blows it out.

I wasn't sure I liked it, though at least I'd managed to get the words *wish* and *hope* in. But it seemed as if a birthday wishing rhyme should be more fun. I just had to try again.

Once I really got into writing, the world sort of disappeared. I didn't look around, I didn't squirm—I didn't even hear anything.

But I did feel Rain elbowing me. "Pixie! Everyone's waiting for you."

I looked up.

"Are you ready?" asked Perrin.

"Um, in a sec." Quickly, I added an exclamation point.

"Now?" Perrin said.

I put down my pencil. "Now."

Perrin flashed her beautiful smile. "Good. I'll recite first." She tucked her pencil behind her ear and began reading from her notebook:

"Happy Birthday, whoever you are
You needn't bother to wish on a star
Just have a big slice of this birthday cake
And hope will help grant the wish you make."

Rain and I began to clap, but no one else joined us. "Don't you think that one's a teeny bit boring,

Cousin?" asked Winnie. I glanced at her in surprise. She was usually so nice.

Perrin's forehead puckered up. "Boring? Let's hear you do better."

"'I'd be happy to." Winnie threw her braid over her shoulder as she took up the challenge.

> "Of all the flavors of cake I've tried
> The hope-filled kind is best
> It tastes like dreams and fantasies
> All sweeter than the rest
> Chocolate's fine, vanilla's nice
> Strawberry shortcake's for me
> But a cake with hope beats all the rest
> Just make your wish and see!"

Picturing those cakes made my mouth water. Winnie's rhyme was delicious! But I couldn't help noticing the disapproving way Nell shook her head.

"It's nice, Winnie dear," she said, "but it's a bit long, isn't it?"

"Who cares how long it is?" snapped Winnie.

"I truly prefer a rhyme that gets right to the point. Like *mine*." Nell opened her notebook and began reading:

> "If you need to pay the rent

A car for mom, a camping tent
Or hope for dad a new career
Just make a wish, it will appear
As long as your request's not greedy
You'll get something that you needy."

Winnie rolled her eyes. "Something that you *need-y?*"

"Yes, indeed-y!" Nell replied.

Rain and I snorted back our laughter. Rhyme time was turning into a poetry slam.

Suddenly Perrin seemed to remember I was there. "Pixie, do you want to read?" she asked. It wasn't really a question.

I looked at the two poems I'd written. I had to decide. My first poem was the kind you'd write for your teacher. But the second was the kind that could make your class crack up. That was the one I decided to read:

"Do you have a dream so fierce
It chews upon your gut
Feeling like a tiny mouse
Is nibbling on a nut?
Then place your hopes upon this cake
And send the mouse away

Just close your eyes and make that wish
Today's your lucky day!"

Rain and Pip giggled. All the other apprentices were smiling, except Perrin. "It's *ni-i-i-c-ce,* Perrin said, drawing out the word. "Though a mouse in the gut is an icky thought. I don't know if your rhyme belongs inside a cake."

"Oh, icky-picky!" exclaimed Pip. "It was fun!"

Perrin's exasperated sigh lifted her bangs off her forehead. She tapped her pencil against the cover of her notebook. She reminded me of Ms. Tomassini when she was trying to be patient. "How about reading yours, Pip?"

"Okey-dokey." Pip smiled a monkey grin that showed every tooth.

"This wishing cake is from the Aunties
If you knew, you'd drop your panties
But a secret it must stay
Just hope you get your wish today!"

"Pippi! You can't put panties in a wishing rhyme!" Perrin exclaimed.

"Why not? They're not actually going to be in the cake," Pip retorted. My mom would have called her sassy.

Suddenly I was imagining old Cone Hat stirring

her big baggy bloomers into the cake batter and I burst out laughing.

"See? Pixie liked it," Pip said.

"I did, too," announced Rain.

Perrin eyed the three of us. I think she was having trouble deciding whether to act like a teacher or to have fun like the students. She settled for a smile and a shake of her head. "O-o-okay. Rainy, read yours," she said.

Rain tugged on her ponytail and began to recite:

"Be kind and fair and you will get

A wish that you will not forget

But if you are a skunk or worse,

I hope instead you'll get a curse!"

"Goose Ladies do not put curses into cakes!"

We all turned to the doorway. "Do you think our mission is a joke, young lady?" Aunt Cone Hat said. "Do you even know what our mission is?"

"To . . . to spread ho . . . hope," Rain stammered.

"Do you think your rhyme will do that?"

"Yes? No?" Rain asked.

Old Cone Hat looked at the grandfather clock. "I assume the rest of you have created verses that are more appropriate. You may all go except Rain, who will have to stay here and create a proper verse."

Rain swiped at her eyes and nodded. Our geese were waiting for us in the front yard. We were supposed to take them to the pond when we were done with rhyme time. But Rain's rhyme hadn't been the only silly one. It didn't seem fair to leave her alone.

"My rhyme was funny, too," I volunteered, because I didn't want Rain to have to stay alone. "We didn't mean to be disrespectful. They were still about granting wishes."

"Well, I'm not at all surprised that *you* were the instigator, Pixie," old Cone Hat snarled. "I told Doris you had a talent for trouble. And now you've proved me right."

CHAPTER THIRTEEN
Ye olde Sock Thief

By the time Rain and I got outside, the other apprentices had disappeared. "They're probably at the pond
with the geese," said Rain. "River and Gray must be
down there with Drizzle and Destiny. Let's go find
them."

"I'll meet you," I said. "I'm going upstairs to get
the eye—I don't think I should keep it any longer. I
have a bad feeling about it."

"What are you going to do with it?"

"I'm going to show it to Aunt Doris."

"Okay." Rain put a hand on my shoulder. "Do you want me to go with you?"

"No, it's my responsibility. I'll see you later, okay?"

Rain began to run down the grassy hill and stopped. "Pixie?"

"Yes?"

"Thanks for being my friend today."

"Sure."

Rain hesitated before she added, "I don't have a friend like you at home. I mean someone close like a best friend."

I was super surprised. "Really? I think you'd make a perfect best friend."

Rain smiled. "Thanks. But if you have a twin, the kids think you're already taken. I guess the other girls don't think I need a best friend."

"Well, Gray's always been my best friend boy. But you're my best friend girl."

"Good." She ran off smiling.

When I got up to our room, I realized someone was already there. It was Pip. She was squatting in front of my chest, rummaging around in my bottom drawer.

I cleared my throat. "What are you looking for?"

"Pixie! I was just going to borrow a pair of socks. All of mine are in the laundry." She held out a foot so I could see her bare ankle above her sneaker.

"Why didn't you ask me?"

"I would've, but then Aunt Espy made you stay behind. I didn't think you'd mind."

I noticed that one of her hands was balled up tight. "What's in your fist?

For a moment I thought she wasn't going to answer. Then she unfurled her fingers. She was holding my locket.

I was so shocked all I could say was, "Why?"

"I found it while I was looking for your socks. It made me wonder what it felt like to have a baby brother. I was going to wear it under my shirt and pretend. It's just been sitting in your drawer, so I didn't think you'd care. I wasn't going to keep it."

It was weird, because instead of sounding sorry, she sounded angry.

"You—you should have asked me." My voice shook as if I were the guilty one.

"Here." Pip held out the locket.

I let it swing on its chain while I thought. Pip had a brother. But Wyatt was a teenager. And he was the only family she had.

"That's okay, you can wear it," I said, taking it and dropping it into her palm. "Just give it back to me tonight. *Okay?*"

"Okay."

She fastened the locket around her neck and headed for the door. "Wait, I thought you wanted socks," I called.

"Never mind. I'll do without them."

I refolded the things in my drawer while I waited for my breathing to return to normal. Something was bothering me besides catching Pip going through my things. I wondered why she hadn't asked to borrow socks when she was getting dressed this morning.

When I was sure she was gone, I pulled out my bottom drawer and found my blue-striped sock ball. Carefully, I put my thumb and forefinger into the center. To my relief, the eye was still there. I plucked it out and placed it on my palm. It glared back at me.

"Stop staring!" I ordered, poking it with my thumb.

I thought I saw it blink.

Yeeeow! I shoved the eye down into the pocket of my shorts and headed back downstairs.

To: Lucy Chang, Alexa Pinkston

Subject: The Latest, Not the Greatest

Destiny has been so bad

Old Cone Hat had a fit

This morning Des made her so mad

That I might have to quit

Later on, we all wrote poems

Tomorrow we'll write more

I haven't made a single cake

This baking camp's a bore!

Love, Pixie

P.S. Here's a dumb goose joke that Wyatt told me:

What birds do you find in Portugal?

Dumb Answer: Portu-geese!

CHAPTER FOURTEEN
Ye olde Family connections

At breakfast I'd heard Aunt Doris tell Aunt Cone Hat that she wanted to check the tires and change the oil in her truck. I knew she kept it parked on the far side of the barn and I was hoping she'd still be there. The secret I'd been keeping was too dangerous. What if I'd put everyone at Chuckling Goose Farm in danger? I had to trust at least one of the Aunts.

Just before I rounded the corner of the barn, I heard two voices, Aunt Doris's and Old Cone Hat's.

Quickly, I hid behind a bale of hay and listened.

"When I stopped by the grocery for cinnamon sticks yesterday, Garrie asked me a strange question," said Aunt Doris. "She wanted to know if we'd found an eyepiece around here."

I'd heard Garrie mentioned before, though I'd never met her. She owned the grocery where the Aunts could get the things they didn't grow themselves.

"An eyepiece? You mean from someone's eyeglasses?" asked Aunt Cone Hat.

"No, an eye from a face. Garrie said she'd been fixing a broken sculpture and that she might have dropped it."

Right away, my heart began going *ka-boing-ka-boing-ka-boing*.

"Here?" old Cone Hat barked.

I heard Aunt Doris snap her gum. "She said it might've fallen out of her pocket during her last delivery."

"That doesn't sound right," muttered Aunt Cone Hat.

For once I agreed with her!

"No, it doesn't," said Aunt Doris. "It sounds more like she's describing something Pixie saw after

Raveneece got shattered. The poor kid told me it gave her nightmares."

"Poor? She's the one that shattered Raveneece!" old Cone Hat grumbled.

"Not on purpose, Espy," Aunt Doris answered calmly. "What I can't figure out is why Garrie would want it. Unless—"

"Unless what? Spit it out, Doris!"

"Unless someone offered to pay her for it," Aunt Doris said. "She's been complaining business is slow."

Aunt Cone Hat's voice became gentler. "Garrie would never have anything to do with Raveneece. We've been friends since the days we were apprentices together. She's ditsy sometimes, but she's not a bad old gal."

"You're probably right," Aunt Doris agreed. "But Pixie told me that after Raveneece cracked, there was a powerful wind that almost blew her back down that hole. She said it made a sweeping sound."

I grabbed onto the hay bale as I remembered the haunting whoosh of that wind. It was a whisking so powerful it might have swept up trees, boulders, graveyards—or me.

"The Broom of Doom!" said Aunt Cone Hat. "I hope you're wrong about that. It was conjured up long ago to put the shattered back together. But what they looked like afterward is less than human. We thought it had been lost."

"I'd heard of it as a girl, but I didn't know it had really existed," whispered Aunt Doris.

Grrrahhh! Aunt Cone Hat let out an angry gargle. "I never should have allowed that little troublemaker to come here."

"But Espy, Pixie is a *descendant*."

"They're all descendants!" thundered Aunt Cone Hat. "Third cousins twice removed . . . eighth cousins once removed. Pixie's no different."

"You know that's not true." Aunt Doris's voice was angry, too.

"You think I could forget? That child's eyes spark when she's riled up, just like my granddaughter Fidelity's did. And her chin's the kind that's always asking for a fight. That's Fidelity's, too." Aunt Cone Hat's voice was suddenly hoarse.

"Yup, she's got plenty of moxie," said Aunt Doris. "I knew you'd love her."

"Love her? I can barely tolerate her!" Espy barked. "My heart was split in two when we lost Fidelity. I never recovered."

"But now you have Pixie, your great-great-

great-granddaughter," said Aunt Doris.

"I DON'T WANT HER!"

"Aw, give the kid a break," Aunt Doris retorted.

For a while the aunts were silent, like wind-up toys that had run down. I remembered the old saying, *"Sticks and stones will break my bones, but words will never hurt me."* But it wasn't true. I felt my heart break a little.

One thing was certain. I wasn't giving the eye to either of them. Before they discovered me, I slipped away and ran for the meadow. In the distance there was a town, and behind it, a row of low, dark hills. They were a long way off, but if I could get there, I'd bury the eye where no one would ever find it. I decided to leave immediately.

Then I crashed into Gray.

CHAPTER FIFTEEN
Ye olde Dumb Plant

Gray was squatting in the grass, feeding Destiny a stalk of pennycress, when I knocked him over like a bowling pin. Destiny flapped out of the way, uninjured. But she scolded me with a few angry honks.

"Gray!" I yelped. "Are you okay? Sorry, I didn't see you." I scooped up Des and smoothed her ruffled feathers.

He looked at me and burped. "I don't know how you could have missed me. Where are you going?" he asked, rolling onto his knees.

I took a quick look around, but everyone was either at the pond or in the farmhouse. "I'm taking a hike."

"What? Where?"

I put Destiny down and pointed toward the shadowy hills. The clouds above them seemed to have gotten darker. "I don't know exactly. Somewhere over there."

"But why, Pix?"

"Because of this." I pulled the evil eye out of my pocket.

Gray took a step backward. "I thought you got rid of it."

"I wanted to, but I just couldn't make myself do it. I mean, it's an eye! Anyway, I can't leave it around here; it's too dangerous. Raveneece might come back for it."

Gray gave the eye another glance. "Could you put that thing away? I feel like it's watching me."

"I know what you mean," I said, slipping it back in my pocket. "But you haven't heard all of the bad news yet, Gray. We're not the only ones who know about it. I heard Aunt Doris tell Aunt Esperanza that someone named Garrie asked about the eye."

Gray sat up. "I've met Garrie! Wyatt, River, and I

stopped at her grocery store for chips and ice cream pops. Wyatt told us she used to be an apprentice here. I guess she flunked out, or quit."

"I think *I* may flunk out," I moaned. "Old Cone Hat hates me. She thinks I never should have come here." I didn't feel like telling him she was my great-great-great-grandmother. It was too painful to admit she didn't want me.

"Huh! I thought old ladies were supposed to be kind and understanding."

"She's not like the others." I yanked up a handful of grass. "But I don't want to keep the eye around here. I'm afraid the Aunts, the apprentices, and the geese could be in danger because of it." I kissed Destiny on top of her sweet head. "I'm going to hide it far away from Chuckling Goose Farm. When I get back, I can send a message to Garrie about where it is. Maybe she'll tell Raveneece. If either of them want it, they can go dig it up."

Gray raised an eyebrow. "I don't know if they'd believe you. And even if they do, they might try to make you come with them to find it."

Ugh! He could be so annoying sometimes. "I didn't say it was the *best* plan," I grumbled.

"Look, whoever dropped the eye here might have

wanted to scare you away, Pix. They probably think it would be easier to steal a wishing cake once you're gone. Or a goose."

Okay, it was a terrible plan, but I was still annoyed. Gray was making me think logically and I didn't want to. But it would be awful if anyone at Chuckling Goose Farm got hurt because of me. I had to stay and find out who'd dropped the eye in the barnyard.

I punched Gray lightly on the arm. "You're a pain, but you can be pretty smart sometimes."

Burp! "I know," Gray answered. "Hey, do you want to come to the little barn with me? I've got to check on one of the hatchlings."

"Sure!" I agreed. He always knew how to cheer me up.

I hadn't had a chance to see the inside of the little barn yet. Compared to the big barn, it looked like a storage shed. But inside were two rooms—one for refrigerating our supply of eggs and the other for incubating and keeping our new hatchlings. I peeked inside the refrigerator. There were at least forty eggs. And they were huge!

In the next room was the incubator where the

chicks were hatched. It was built like a cupboard with a temperature gage and a window on the door. When I peered through, I saw shelves covered with straw where the fertilized eggs rested. A fan at the top spun gently. I knew it was for circulating air over and under the eggs.

"I guess this one's more scientific than the one my dad made out of an old fish tank when Destiny was still an egg," I said.

Gray nodded. "Wait till you see the brooder."

Destiny's "brooder" had been my brother's old playpen. But this one resembled a wooden sandbox with wire over it. The floor was covered in wood shavings, feathers, and straw. Four tiny, fuzzy goslings were peeping and pecking. A fifth gosling, slightly bigger, was standing by itself.

"I can hardly remember Des being this size," I said. "They're adorable. But what's the bigger one doing in there?"

"Oh, that's Dewey," Gray said. He opened the wire cage door and the little goose came hobbling over. Gray lifted it out and snuggled it. "Dewey's got bumblefoot."

"What's that?"

Gently, Gray took the gosling's foot and turned it

so I could see a pink bump on the underside. "It's an infection on his foot pad. He stepped on something and it got infected."

"Poor Dewey! I know what that feels like," I said, rubbing the little guy's head. "Will he be okay?"

"I hope so. We wash it every day and put an antibiotic on it." Gray's forehead was wrinkled with worry. "The ganders—males—fight over the females. That's why we only keep a couple of them. Dewey was supposed to be sent to another farm. But since he's injured, he's here indefinitely. Maybe he'll get to stay."

I knew it was what Gray wanted. "Maybe you'll be a veterinarian someday," I said. "You could specialize in geese and golden retrievers." In fifth grade Gray had been obsessed with a golden retriever puppy that belonged to one of our classmates.

"Ha-ha," he said. But he looked pretty pleased.

CHAPTER SIXTEEN
Ye olde Thankless Job

On my first cake-baking day I woke up before the sun rose. After I'd washed and dressed, I mashed down the top of my hair with barrettes and pulled the rest back in a tight ponytail. I didn't want a single strand getting into the cake batter. I was determined not to do anything that would make Aunt Cone Hat mad.

The kitchen was deserted when I got downstairs, but I knew it wouldn't be for long. As quickly and quietly as I could, I set the table with thirteen of everything: placemats, plates, bowls, napkins, utensils, and glasses. Next I climbed a stepstool to search the top cabinets for serving bowls, platters, and a vase. While I was poking around, I found exactly what I needed.

In a dark corner, sitting behind some empty jam jars, was a yellow sugar bowl with a cracked top. Someone had glued the pieces of the lid back together, but I guess Aunt Cone Hat hadn't liked how it looked, because the sugar bowl she used now was white and had a matching milk pitcher. I checked behind me before I pulled out the old one and lifted the lid. The little yellow bowl was still half full of sugar, though it had a hard crust. She must have forgotten about it long ago.

Perfect.

I poked my finger through the crust, dug a hole in the sugar, and dropped in Raveneece's eye. Sprinkling sugar back over it made me feel queasy. It was a relief to put the lid on again and push the sugar bowl back into its dark corner.

Hurriedly, I chose a fruit bowl, grabbed a pair of kitchen scissors, and slipped out the back door. The morning air was cool and the blueberries in the kitchen garden, which Aunt Cone Hat called a "potager," were still moist with dew. I picked enough to fill my bowl, and cut daisies and Sweet William for a bouquet. By the time the sun came up over the distant hills, I felt calmer—so calm I imagined those hills were singing to me. But as it got louder, I realized the song was coming from *inside* the house. Someone was singing "Climb Ev'ry Mountain" in a voice that sounded like a goose singing opera.

With my arms full of goodies, I used my backside to push the door open again. "Climb Ev'ry Mountain" grew louder. I took two steps backward and—*YOWCH*! Something snapped my backside! Even through my jean shorts, it really hurt.

"It's you!" exclaimed Aunt Cone Hat as I whirled around. She grabbed the bowl before I dropped it, but the flowers I'd picked fell to the ground. She was wearing a fuzzy purple bathrobe and matching fuzzy slippers, but she still had her cone hat on. The only thing that kept me from laughing was the pain the mean-looking creature standing beside her had caused.

"Th—there's a goose in the kitchen," I stammered. "I thought they weren't allowed."

Old Coney narrowed her eyes at me. "It's the apprentices who aren't supposed to be here at this hour."

I wondered if she'd made up that rule just for me. "I couldn't sleep, so I came down to help with breakfast." I glared at the goose while I rubbed my aching bottom.

"I'm sorry you got goose-bit, but La Blanca thinks she's a watchdog. She doesn't take kindly to intruders."

But I wasn't an intruder, and Aunt Cone Hat didn't sound sorry at all. "Was that you singing 'Climb Ev'ry Mountain'?" I asked.

She nodded. The mountain on her head rocked dangerously. "Singing is good exercise for the lungs."

"My mom runs a chorus at the senior residence where she works. She sings it with her ladies."

I caught a flicker of interest in Aunt Cone Hat's eyes. But she said, "I don't have time for conversation."

"I'll wash the berries and leave," I muttered, reaching for the bowl.

La Blanca hissed at me again.

"Hush, Blankie. Bad goosey!" scolded Aunt Cone Hat, but she said it more gently than she ever spoke to me.

I stood there and watched that big, spoiled goose eat every last petal on the flowers I'd dropped.

"You can pick some more later." Old Coney put

her hands on her hips and studied me. "What else were you planning to serve for breakfast?"

I gulped back the lump in my throat before I could answer. "Toast with jam. Cereal with blueberries."

"In this kitchen, we don't serve cold cereal. What else can you cook?"

"Macaroni with squeeze cheese and hot dogs, but I think that's better for lunch or dinner." I finally got up the courage to look at her. She was eyeing me as if I had something gross stuck in my teeth. "My mom usually does the cooking. Her French toast is my favorite," I said quietly.

"Do you want to learn how to make French toast?"

"Um, sure."

"Get a half-dozen eggs from the refrigerator and crack them into that bowl." She pointed to a silver soup tureen that was big enough for Destiny to swim in. "And make sure you don't get even a sliver of shell in there. I'm going to get dressed and drop La Blanca at the barn."

"Yes, Aunt Esperanza," I said, fighting to keep my voice steady.

"Make sure you're finished by the time I get back." She walked out of the room, her purple slippers slapping the floor with each step.

I was used to helping my mom in the kitchen, but at home we used chicken eggs. Goose eggs are about twice as big as a chicken's and heavier, too. I held my breath each time I cracked one. Somehow I managed to keep the shell bits out. Then I cut some more flowers from the garden and placed them in an empty honey jar I'd filled with water.

When Aunt Cone Hat returned, she handed me a long loaf of bread and a huge knife to slice it with. At home my parents would never have trusted me with such a big blade. I felt like a knight, getting her first sword—proud and a little dangerous.

Once I finished, I dipped each slice into a mixture of eggs, milk, honey, and cinnamon. Aunt Cone Hat fried them in butter on a big griddle pan.

"Run back upstairs now and don't tell anyone you were in here this morning," she said when we were finished. "I don't want everyone thinking they can just barge into my kitchen whenever they want."

She didn't even thank me. I guess it was dumb of me to think she would.

I was pulling the door shut behind me when she called, "Pixie! Come back tomorrow morning, same time. Don't be late!"

CHAPTER SEVENTEEN
Ye olde Baking Secrets

After breakfast and a quick rhyming session, we had a break for goose playtime. Gray and River were responsible for getting the geese down to the pond. I ran upstairs to get one of Destiny's favorite toys, a long red ribbon decorated with jingle bells that Mom had made for her. Des loved a good game of tug-of-war, even if the ribbon was tied to a chair. She'd yank and yank, making the bells go crazy.

There were eighteen geese at Chuckling Goose

Farm. Most of them were paddling in the pond or dabbling in the tall grasses. But a few curious ones came to hear Des play her bells. I recognized one of them right away.

"Here comes trouble wearing feathers," I said to Gray.

He followed my gaze and laughed. "You mean La Blanca? She's not so bad. Her honk is worse than her bite."

"Yeah, unless she bites *you*." I explained about helping in the kitchen, even though old Coney had warned me not to tell anyone. I could keep a secret better than almost anyone, but I was feeling spiteful.

"It's not right that she lets La Blanca in the kitchen when the others aren't allowed," I grumbled. "Did you know she calls her Blankie?"

Gray sent me a sideways smirk. "I guess Destiny isn't the only spoiled goose around here. And just so you know, Des and Blankie are buddies."

As if to prove it, La Blanca waddled closer and took the other end of the ribbon in her beak. Gray let go of his end, so the two geese could shake the bells and their cute, feathered bottoms. "They're like a girl band," Gray hooted, "the Ding Dongs!" He shoved me with a shoulder.

"Ha-ha!" I shoved him back. I was glad Des had made a friend, but why did it have to be La Blanca?

"You know, if you don't want to help with breakfast, you shouldn't do such a good job," Gray advised me. "That French toast was delicious. But next time, get some eggshell in the batter. Then Coney will fire you."

"Nah, if I make her mad, she might not let me bake any wishing cakes. I can't wait to see how that's done."

"Yeah. The guys aren't allowed in on that. But I can't wait until delivery day. Wyatt says it's like being a secret agent. You get to see the apprentices using their special powers, too."

"I know. It's going to be cool," I agreed. But I couldn't see how my secret power would be useful. Freezing a birthday person so I could deliver a birthday cake would be extremely extreme.

After Des and La Blanca finished their musical performance, we followed them around while they searched the grass for pennycress and other favorite weeds. It was funny how they tested each plant for tenderness, like shoppers in the produce aisle. Gray plucked a long strand of tasseled grass and chewed it the way I'd seen Wyatt do.

When I heard clanging coming from the farm-house, I swiveled around. It was Aunt Fancy, strik-ing the big triangle that hung on the porch.

"I guess it's time for baking," I said. "See you later, Gray. Bye, Destiny!" For a moment she looked up at me, but she didn't try to follow. Instead she and La Blanca went back to munching. It made my heart feel a little lighter.

After we washed up, Rain and I hurried to the din-ing room. The older apprentices were already seated at the table. Each of them had a large spoon on a cord or ribbon, dangling from around her neck like a strange necklace. The spoons were all differ-ent. Perrin's was silver and had a long handle with a heart-shaped bowl. Winnie's spoon had a pearly handle and a shell-shaped bowl. The handle on Nell's looked like a stem and its bowl was shaped like the head of a daisy. And Pip's spoon had a handle like a giant, old-fashioned key.

I was wondering where they'd gotten those amaz-ing spoons when Aunt Cone Hat marched into the dining room with Fancy, Bernie, and Doris right behind her. The Aunts were all wearing crisp white aprons over billowy black dresses, as if today were a special occasion.

Aunt Cone Hat took her seat at the head of the table and plopped a fat book in front of her. It was covered in old, yellowed fabric that might once have been a flour sack and was stamped with designs of cakes—tall ones, flat ones, swirly ones, sloppy ones, and one with about twenty layers that looked like they were about to tumble.

"This cookbook was handwritten by Mother Goose herself," she said, looking at Rain and me. "Every recipe we use is inside. There are more than enough to make a different cake every day of the year if we wanted to, though we repeat our customer's favorites quite often." She stopped and sipped some water from a jelly jar glass. It gave me a chance to breathe, which I'd hardly been doing because I was so excited.

"But a person can't become an expert baker simply by reading a book," Aunt Esperanza continued. "Like so many things, baking must be learned by observing and—*are you listening, Pixie?*"

"Yes!" I answered, jumping in my seat. But I'd also been looking at the bib of her apron where an amazing spoon was hanging. The handle was a goose's head, the stem was its neck, and the bowl was its round, feathered body. Although the silver it was made of looked old, the goose seemed almost alive.

Old Cone Hat sniffed. "Over time you'll develop a good eye, a good nose, and wrists that can coax a batter to cooperate. Of course, you will also need a pleasing rhyme and a good heart." She raised an eyebrow at Rain and me. "Just remember that batters are sensitive. Some can be temperamental and others can be easygoing, but all are secretive by nature. Whatever happens between you and the bowl is private."

I'd stirred cake batters for Mom before, but they hadn't shown any more personality than cottage cheese. "Excuse me, but how can you tell what a bowl of batter is feeling?" I asked.

Aunt Esperanza's nostrils flared so wide they looked like bat caves. "If you'd been paying attention, you would have heard me say 'baking must be learned by observing.'"

"Sorry, I guess I've got first-day jitters," I mumbled.

The old grump stroked her goose spoon like a pet. "Before we begin today's baking, your aunts and cousins have each prepared a baking tip for you new girls. We'll go around the table." She poked Aunt

Bernie in the shoulder with her bony finger. "Bern, you start."

Aunt Bernie pointed her scratched silver spoon at us. "The first thing we do is line up the ingredients and the baking implements. It's important to have everything at hand."

Aunt Fancy was next. "We always read a recipe through twice before we begin. That way, we don't leave anything out." The handle of her spoon was studded with glittering purple jewels that looked like amethysts.

"We never take shortcuts," continued Perrin. "We follow every step."

"If you're happy on baking day, your cake will be light and sweet," said Winnie. "So you must think of happy things."

"And if you're worried or sad on baking day, your cake will flop," said Nell. Then she bit a fingernail.

"When the cakes are in the oven, don't shout, jump, or laugh," said Pip. "That makes the cakes grouchy."

"How do you know when a cake is grouchy?" I asked.

"Oh, you'll know," replied Pip.

Aunt Doris was the last to speak. "Have fun on your first baking day, kiddos." She winked at Rain and me. "I can still remember mine." The handle of her spoon had a tiny replica of her truck at the end.

Aunt Esperanza walked to the big cabinet on the side of the room. "Every Goose Girl gets her own mixing spoon," she said. "If you treat it well and use it wisely, it will help you coax the batter to obey you." She took a key from her pocket and beckoned to Rain and me. "Come here, girls."

We slipped off the bench and padded over to her. I think I could hear both our hearts beating as she unlocked the top drawer. The older girls murmured with excitement. I guess they were remembering their own "spoon days."

From deep in the drawer, Aunt Cone Hat removed a cloth bundle. It was powder blue and looked as soft as a baby's blanket. As gently as if it held a real baby, she set the bundle on top of the cabinet.

"Rain, you first," she said, unrolling the cloth partway.

My heart melted at the sight of Rain's spoon. It was silver with a handle that widened just enough to fit easily in her palm. But the real treasure was its bowl, which was shaped like an open book. The cover was slightly cupped for mixing or tasting, and it was open to a page with words etched into the silver. I leaned over Rain's shoulder to read them:

Call upon hope
Rhyme recite
Mix in wish
Bake it right!

I felt envious watching Aunt Cone Hat tie the spoon's black silken cord around Rain's neck. I couldn't help wishing it had been mine. Still, I gave Rain a hug before she went back to sit with the other girls. I knew if I'd gotten the book spoon, she'd have been happy for me.

"All right, Pixie, you're next," said Aunt Esperanza in the grouchy voice she always used for me. But I wanted a spoon of my own so badly I didn't care. When she began unrolling the rest of the cloth, I sucked in my breath like I was slurping spaghetti. I kept holding it when she stopped to flex her cramped fingers. By the time she was on the last fold, I was feeling light-headed.

My spoon was not elegant, or charming, or fun. It was wooden. It was stumpy. Its bowl had a burnt spot. There wasn't a hint of design on the front or back.

I gulped back my disappointment and whispered, "Thank you, Aunt."

"Turn around."

I took a deep breath while she tied it on my neck—
and caught a whiff of something fragrant and spicy.
"Cinnamon!" I murmured.

The hint of a smile appeared on Aunt Cone Hat's
face. Or maybe it was a smirk.

"Okay, girls. Off to the kitchen," she ordered.

CHAPTER EIGHTEEN
Ye olde Bratty Batter

Six places had been set atop the kitchen's big cooking island. Each one had a bowl, a mixing cup, measuring spoons, and a neatly folded white apron. The ingredients—flour, sugar, spices, and a lot of other stuff—were neatly organized in the center, along with tools like whisks and spatulas. Maybe Aunt Bernie was the one who'd done that. I looked around for her, but none of the aunts were in the kitchen.

Perrin was tying on her apron. "Where are they?" I asked.

"Who?"

"The Goose Ladies. Why aren't they here?"

"Oh, they're watching movies, practicing yoga, reading, doing whatever they like. Aunt Doris is probably out for a drive."

Rain and I sent each other wide-eyed looks.

"But isn't this their job?" I exclaimed.

"I thought that they would help us," Rain added, more politely.

Perrin put an arm around each of us. "Oh, girls, we've all been so busy, I guess no one remembered to explain. During most of the year, the Aunts bake cakes that they sell to stores. They're called Every Day's Your Birthday cakes. Though they don't grant wishes, people love them. That's how the Goose Ladies earn the money they use to run this farm and how they can afford to bake wishing cakes, which, as you know, they give away."

"They are awfully old to be doing all that work," said Rain.

"You're right about that," Winnie agreed. "That's why it's so important for the apprentices to come here each summer. In order to keep our heritage alive, we descendants of Mother Goose must learn the Goose Ladies' secrets. And while you're here, the Aunts get a much-deserved break. Think of it this way:

"To accomplish your best

It's important to rest

For working when weary

Can make your cake dreary."

"Shouldn't it be the other way around, though?" I asked. "Shouldn't the Aunts be the ones making magical cakes, while we make the everyday ones?"

Perrin smiled. "I asked that exact same thing when I first arrived here. But since a Goose Girl's power is strongest in her youth, your magic is more powerful than theirs. That's one reason why the apprentices bake the wishing cakes. But there's something even more important. The Aunts are worried that their real purpose, keeping hope in the world, is dying out. They're counting on some of us to return to Chuckling Goose Farm when we've finished with school."

"Do you mean to become Aunts?" I asked. I was trying to imagine myself in a billowy black skirt and a cone hat.

"Yes," replied Perrin. "What could be more important than keeping hope alive in the world?"

"Will you be coming back here, Perrin?" asked Rain.

Perrin's eyes grew moist. "I've been coming here for five years and I'm still not sure. I love Chuckling Goose! But I've always wanted to be a kindergarten teacher."

"What about you, Winnie?" I asked. "Do you think you'll be a Goose Lady?"

"Not exactly," said Winnie, without having to think about it. "My mother is a doctor in town. She comes here to treat the Aunts, whenever they need her. I'd like to do that, too. That way I can keep an eye on them and help out in the kitchen occasionally." She came around behind Rain and then me to tie our apron strings.

"That sounds like a good plan," I said. But inside I felt a little worried. What if none of the apprentices decided to stay? Would it be the end of the Goose Ladies?

"Okay," said Perrin when she'd finished my bow. "We'd better get started."

"I don't think I remember all the baking rules," I admitted.

"Don't worry. Just watch us," said Perrin. She tapped her spoon against the counter. "One, two, three!

"Mix and chatter, mix and chatter

That's the way to coax a batter
If a pleasing rhyme you say
Your request it will obey."

The goose girls repeated the rhyme three times, so by the third, Rain and I could say it, too. Then Perrin pulled a stack of index cards from her apron pocket and handed one to each of us. Mine was a recipe for angel food cake, written out in neat block letters.

"Just take it one step at a time," said Perrin before getting to work on her own cake.

Remembering Aunt Fancy's advice, I read my card through twice before I began cracking eggs. Thanks to Aunt Cone Hat, I could do it with my eyes closed.

Soon the kitchen was noisy with whisking, beating, scraping, and the rumbling and sighing of our big oven. It wasn't long before I'd measured all the ingredients into my bowl. Out of the corner of my eye, I saw Perrin remove the mixing spoon from her neck and open her rhyming notebook. One by one the others did the same.

"Rain, watch this!" I whispered, nodding toward Perrin.

Rain raised her head just in time to catch Perrin placing one hand over her heart. Then she dipped her mixing spoon into the bowl.

While she stirred, Perrin glanced at her notebook and recited her wishing rhyme. Her voice was the kind you'd use to coax a reluctant five-year-old to obey.

"Happy Birthday, whoever you are
    You needn't bother to wish on a star . . . "

I'd already heard the poem on rhyming day. But now I thought Winnie had been right. It was a little boring. The truth was, so far baking day was pretty much like baking with my mom. Nice, but no big whoop. I couldn't help feeling a little disappointed.

"I hope I don't drop my notebook into the bowl," Rain joked.

"Me, either!" I took a deep breath and removed my spoon from around my neck. Copying Perrin, I pressed my hand over my heart. "Come on, Stumpy, let's mix up this batter," I muttered, plopping the homely old spoon into my bowl. I glanced at the wishing rhyme I'd scribbled into my notebook and began reciting:

"You cannot drink an ocean
    You can't build a mountain from sand
    But any type of wish you make
    Will fit inside your hand—"

"Baw-wing!"

Had I just heard someone say *boring?* I looked around. The rest of the girls were busy talking to their bowls.

"Twy again!" the voice demanded. It was squeaky and bubbly, the way a goldfish might sound if a goldfish could talk. It seemed to be coming from the bowl.

"You cannot drink an ocean—" I began.

"No! No! I don' wike dat one!" The batter rippled around the edges.

My heart began to thump. I glared into the bowl and caught a glimpse of a face. It had eyes like two straight lines, circles for cheeks, and a pouty mouth.

"Y-you can talk?" I stammered.

"Bedda den you can wite."

"How would you know?" I grumbled. "You're a bowl of batter, not a writing teacher."

The batter stuck out its tongue, which looked like a lump. It made me so mad, I began mixing faster.

The face began to fade.

"Wait! Who are you?" I yelped.

But there was no reply. Desperately, I began turning the pages of my notebook until I found a rhyme that might work. I recited it to the bowl in a perky, totally embarrassing voice:

"A swimming pig or a flying snake

No matter how weird

A wish you make

It might come true on your birthday cake

Just hope your wish isn't a mistake!"

"Flying snake, ha-ha. Make it maw *funny!"* I heard as the face reappeared.

"O-o-okay . . . hold on a sec." I wracked my brains, trying to figure out what a cake batter would think was funny. I decided to go with the kind of rhyme my little brother would like.

"Tickle tickle with my spoon

Jump up over Mr. Moon

I hope you'll take my wish with you

And ask Sir Moon to make it true."

While I said the rhyme, I stirred the batter lightly. I hoped it would feel like a tickle.

"Hoo-hoo, hoo-hoo!" The batter popped a bubble and the face disappeared.

"Wait! What about my wish?" I stirred the batter, trying to make the face return. Instead, I saw crinkly eyes . . . a bumpy nose . . . a smile like half an orange . . . and a pointy hat with a round brim. I knew who that face belonged to.

"Cheers for the girl with the cinnamon curl
Who protects wishes with a will so strong
Villains and thugs better scatter like bugs
For the spoon she wields will banish wrong."

"Mother Goose? Is that you?" I squeaked as if I'd suddenly become a mouse.

"Of course! I'm so glad Esperanza has given my spoon to you. How do you like it, dear?"

Holy goose! I had her spoon!

"It smells super good, like cinnamon," I said.

"That's because I got it from a peddler who'd traveled through India, where cinnamon trees grow

"W-was your rhyme about me?" I stammered.

"Didn't you like it?"

"Yes, but I don't really deserve it."

"But you will someday."

"I hope so," I murmured. "I—I don't think the batter likes me or my rhymes very much. I'm afraid I'm going to fail wishing cakes."

Mother Goose chuckled and the batter rippled. "Oh, not at all! The batter imps like to tease. But they will always honor your wishes, for I have instructed them to do so."

"But why?"

"Because you have my spoon. And because your heart is braver than brave and truer than true. Just like your great-great-great-grandmother. You two must take good care of each other." Suddenly the batter became a whirlpool like the kind that makes ships disappear in the ocean and Mother Goose's voice grew very faint. "Hurry and get this cake in the oven!" she called. There was a sharp, sucking sound and a *POP!* Mother Goose disappeared.

My heart was beating so fast, I had trouble filling the baking pans without spilling the batter. Finally, I joined the end of the line of girls waiting for the oven. Perrin stood at the oven door, wearing thick red mitts to protect her hands while she slid our pans carefully onto the racks. She'd just wedged my cake in with the others when Aunt Bernie and Aunt Fancy entered the kitchen.

"Noon—time for lunch, girls," announced Bernie. "We'll babysit your cakes, so they won't burn."

"There are sandwiches and cookies on the dining room table," Fancy told us. "Be back at two for frosting."

Before I left, I gave Stumpy a careful cleaning with a soft, damp towel. It no longer looked ugly to me. Instead, it reminded me of my dad's hands,

which were weathered and scarred by hard work. I
hung it on a hook with the rest of the spoons. Even
among all that silver, it looked noble.

"See you later, *Sir Stumpy*," I promised.

CHAPTER NINETEEN
ye olde Quality control

On my way out the kitchen door, I bumped into Aunt Doris. "Sorry!" I exclaimed.

"Hey kiddo, I've been waiting for you," she said, leading me to a bench in the empty hall. "How was baking?"

We sat down and looked at each other. I had the feeling she wanted to know who or what I'd seen in my batter and I was dying to tell her. But we both knew that information was supposed to be private. Didn't being truer than true also mean sticking to the Goose Ladies' rules?

"It was interesting," I said.

"Okay." Aunt Doris smiled. "I want to talk to you about quality control."

"Did I do something wrong?"

"No, kiddo," she said, waving a hand to chase away the thought. "It's just that when you make a product, whether it's toothpaste or mosquito repellant, you have to know if it's doing its job. The same is true for wishing cakes. The thing is, you can tell if your toothpaste is working by looking at your smile in the mirror. And you can tell if your mosquito repellent is working if you don't get bitten. But since we never know who gets a wishing cake, we can't check our work."

I thought for a moment. "So how do you know?"

Aunt Doris lowered her head so we were nose to nose. "We test it."

"You mean you and the other Aunts make wishes?"

"No, kiddo, the new goose girls do. We let you try one out on your birthday."

For a moment I couldn't speak. "My birthday is in two weeks and a day—July twenty-second," I said.

Aunt Doris cracked her gum. "I know! That's why I'm telling you now. You need time to decide what you're going to wish."

I hesitated for a moment before I asked, "Does everyone wish for world peace? Or an end to hunger?"

"Oh, kiddo, no wish is strong enough to do that. Great problems can only be solved by small steps. Like donating to a food pantry is a step toward solving hunger. And building an inclusive playground is a step toward bringing a community together." She took my hand and gave it a squeeze. "But it's okay to wish for personal things, too."

"Did you get to wish on a cake when you were an apprentice?" I asked.

"Yup."

"What did you wish for?"

Aunt Doris blushed. I'd never seen her do that before. "A year's supply of bubble gum," she admitted.

"And what did you get?"

"Cavities! Lots of them."

We both burst out laughing.

"I'm starving, how about you?" Aunt Doris asked after she'd caught her breath.

"Yup," I said.

"Okay, race you to the dining room!" Before I was on my feet, she was off and running.

It wasn't fair, but it was fun.

* * *

On my way to meet Gray in the meadow, I thought about things to wish for. My two top choices used to be a baby brother and a golden retriever puppy, but now I had Sammy. And although Destiny was a goose, I couldn't imagine having another pet I loved as much.

I'd also longed for a modern bathroom with a fancy shower instead of the claw-foot tub we had at home. But now that I was at Chuckling Goose Farm, I kind of missed the old bathtub. Lately the only thing I'd wished for was straight, silky hair like Perrin's. My hair made me look like a guinea pig was sitting on my head. (Really! There's a kind of guinea pig called a Texel that has crazy, curly cinnamon hair.)

I knew what my friends at home would wish for—Alexa Pinkston would want to paint her room because every room in her house was pink and she was longing for a different color. My friend Lucy Chang could have used something to cuddle. Since she gave away the History Village Dolls she loved, either a kitten or a little sister would be perfect for her.

I thought maybe Gray would wish for a tool bench like my dad's. More than anything, he loved to help fix things around the estate we lived on.

As for my dad, well, I knew he could use a week off. Being the caretaker at a big estate meant our family never got to go on vacation. I thought Mom would like that, too, though she might wish for a new sewing machine to help make the costumes she loved. Her old one was cranky and sometimes it took days before Dad could get around to fixing it.

When you could have almost anything you wanted, it made wishing for something really hard.

CHAPTER TWENTY
Ye olde Disappointment

After I left Aunt Doris, I met Gray for a picnic in the back meadow. He'd brought both Destiny and La Blanca with him. The two geese had quickly become inseparable, which was probably why Des didn't run away to find me anymore. But he'd also brought Dewey! The little gosling was walking better, though he didn't wander far from Gray.

"Dewey looks as if he's improved a lot," I said.

"A bit. He still needs more time in the little barn." Gray scooted closer. "I've been introducing him to our ganders, Commander and Alexander, in short spurts. "I always feed them something tasty to make them think happy thoughts about being with him."

"It's great that you're helping him," I said.

"I wish I could do more," Gray said. "It's hard, 'cause we're busy all the time. This morning we milked Fern and Ivy. Then we raked out their stalls and replaced the old hay with clean stuff. Next we did the same thing for Thomas. The hay bales are stored up in the loft and we had to get a few of them down. But look!" He pulled his right sleeve up above his bicep. "Muscles!"

"Where?" I asked, curling my fingers like binoculars to examine his arm. "You mean those freckles?"

"Ha-ha! Very funny." He took a giant bite out of his sandwich.

I waited until we finished eating before revealing my secret. I knew he would go a little crazy and I didn't want him to choke to death. When I finally did tell him, he scooped up Dewey and did a happy dance.

"You're getting a wishing cake? That's fantastically, amazingly, awesomely, astonishingly, incredibly, outstandingly, extraordinarily, monumentally c-r-a-z-y! We've got to start planning what you'll wish for, like a hoverboard or a bearded dragon, or—" Gray stopped jumping for a moment. "Or did you already decide?"

"I think so," I said, though I suddenly realized how boring my wish would sound to him. "I thought I'd wish for a family beach vacation. Mom and Dad both work so hard they could use one. I know Mom would love to collect shells for craft projects. Dad could stretch out in the sun and sing along to those corny eighties songs he listens to. You know how Sammy loves to dig holes. And I'll ask for you to come with us."

"But Pix—you could go see grizzlies in Alaska or take a kayak down the Colorado rapids!"

"That's what you'd want." I sighed. "You know, deciding isn't easy. I've been thinking about so many things, my brain hurts."

"Then maybe you should give your wish to someone else." Gray grinned at me.

It was my turn to laugh. But suddenly I was worried. "Aren't you having fun here?"

He nudged me with his bony shoulder. "Come on, I was just kidding. This place is great. It's fun, even when we're working. And tomorrow, we're going to sneak around delivering wishing cakes. I can't wait!"

"Me, either," I agreed, jumping up. "But I'd better get back to the kitchen now. We're learning about frosting this afternoon. I don't want to give Aunt Cone Hat a reason to ground me.

"Bye, Dessie." I leaned over and kissed her soft little head. Then I realized La Blanca was staring at me. "Um, bye, Blankie," I said.

She took a step closer to me.

"I'm not kissing you," I told her.

Suddenly she thrust her head at my knee.

I inhaled sharply, expecting a bite. But she only nudged me.

"You want a pat?" I asked, reaching out to her cautiously. "Don't bite my fingers," I warned. "I need them for baking."

And she didn't. Instead of biting, that big, bad goose wriggled her rear in a happy dance.

Back in the kitchen, Aunt Fancy was in charge. She was the cake-decorating expert at Chuckling Goose. She divided us into pairs and assigned each team a frosting. Rain and I got whipped cream, which was the easiest. All it took were three ingredients—heavy cream, powdered sugar, and vanilla—and a lot of beating with a whisk. Aunt Fancy didn't believe in

using an electric beater. "It's important to stay con-
nected to your cake every step of the way," she told
us. "You have to feel the movement in your wrist and
watch how the ingredients respond."

Rain and I took turns whisking until the frosting
began to form peaks that looked like new snow on a
sledding hill. By the time it was done, our wrists felt
like we'd sprained them in a sledding accident. We
used a spatula that looked a lot like a butter knife
to spread the frosting over our cakes. Rain came up
with our decorating idea, a circle of flowers we made
by cutting strawberries into petals and placing a
mini chocolate chip in each center.

I was feeling pretty proud until I looked at the
older girls' work. Their cakes were like paintings.
Perrin and Nell had used their frosting to create a
woodland world of birds, squirrels, and rabbits peek-
ing out from behind trees. Winnie and Pip's cake
had mountains and a realistic waterfall. Aunt Fancy
had made a day-and-night cake, half sunny blue sky
and half starry night. I guess it represented the perfect day. Suddenly flowers seemed really boring.

To write "Happy Birthday," the apprentices used
plastic frosting bags with piping tips, which was sort
of like using a squeeze bottle of mustard to write

on a hot dog. Their lettering was even and beautiful. I couldn't even write that way with a pencil and paper. But Aunt Fancy showed Rain and me how to use a stencil to press the outline of the words into our cake. Then we used a chopstick dipped in green frosting to go over the imprint we'd made.

"Everyone started this way," Aunt Fancy assured us. "It's like using training wheels. Just be sure to leave enough room for the birthday person's name."

"But if the cakes go to random people, how can we know their names?" I asked.

"We don't," Aunt Fancy said. "The names appear on the cakes after they're delivered."

I could tell there was another magical rhyme coming, so I took out my notebook. I was worried that I wouldn't remember the ones I'd already learned.

"It's short," Aunt Fancy said as if she knew what I was thinking. "Just repeat after me.

"When this wish cake finds its home
Make the receiver's identity known
Top and center the name will appear
Written in icing, neat and clear."

It made me think of a story my dad had told about something that happened when he was a kid. He'd loved magic, so he'd gotten a book from the library that explained how to do tricks. One of them was making invisible ink. He began by dipping a Q-tip into lemon juice, and writing a message to his brother on a sheet of paper: "Hello, Dumbhead!"

When it dried, the message disappeared. Later he gave his brother, my Uncle Bobby, the "blank" paper and told him that magic words would appear if he held it over a light bulb. The paper was supposed to darken from the bulb's heat, except for the lemon juice writing, which would stay cooler and stand out. Instead, the paper caught fire! Quickly Uncle Bobby poured his glass of grape juice over it, which left a big stain on the rug in their room. When my grandparents discovered it, Dad and Uncle Bobby didn't get any dessert for a week.

But the names on our wishing cakes weren't written in advance. The magic was real. Boy, would my dad have liked to see that!

"All right, girls, I think that's enough for today," said Aunt Fancy. "Tomorrow morning when the sun comes up, you'll be setting off with your deliveries." She looked down at her notes.

"Nell and River will go north with me. Pip and Gray will go south with Aunt Doris. Winnie and Rain will go east with Aunt Bernie. And Perrin and

Wyatt will go west on their own." Aunt Fancy looked up and smiled at Perrin. "We've agreed you're ready. But I'm expecting you to make sure Wyatt doesn't speed!"

Perrin clutched her spoon and beamed.

"Don't be late tomorrow!" Aunt Fancy's bracelets jingled as she shooed everyone off with a pink polka-dot dish towel.

"Wait! You forgot me!" I exclaimed.

Aunt Fancy's smile drooped. "Oh, Pixie, you won't be going. Aunt Esperanza wants you to stay here with her. She asked me to tell you to come down extra early to help with breakfast."

CHAPTER TWENTY-ONE
Ye olde Writing on the Wall

I pounded up to the second floor, where the Aunts had their rooms, determined to find Aunt Doris. But when I got to the row of closed doors, I felt nervous about knocking. I had no idea which room was hers, and I didn't want Aunt Cone Hat popping out like a skeleton in a scary movie.

I'd nearly given up when I heard a gum crack from behind the door opposite the stairs. I only had to tap once.

"Hey, kiddo, come on in," said Aunt Doris as she opened the door.

At first, her large, square room seemed ordinary. On one side was a neatly made bed with a cherry red blanket that matched the curtains on her window. The other side of the room was set up like an ordinary office, with a desk, a chair, a bookcase, and a table for her computer and printer. But her walls were covered in writing from top to bottom. There was even writing on the ceiling! I nearly tripped over a stepladder as I tried to read it. The print was really small.

She handed me a magnifying glass. "Take your time and look closely, kiddo."

It was a while before I realized I was looking at dates and addresses. It looked like a crazy mess until I realized they were grouped by month.

"There aren't any names," I said, running my fingers down a column. And suddenly, I knew. "This is the list! It's how you deliver the cakes without knowing who's getting them, isn't it?"

"Yup."

"But where did you get them?"

She waved a hand at the walls. "Oh, we have helpers. Former Goose Ladies who work in town halls, hospitals, schools, libraries, dental offices—and everywhere else records are kept."

"Wow, Goose Lady spies!"

"Oh, kiddo, you're a riot," said Aunt Doris. "But these days, Bernie and I deliver most of our wishing cakes to stores and bakeries. We mix them in with the regular orders and count on people buying the fanciest ones for their relatives and friends who are having birthdays."

"But what about the magic!" I exclaimed. "I thought the Goose Ladies used their powers to deliver wishing cakes."

Aunt Doris put a hand on my shoulder. "The truth is, there aren't enough of us anymore to use magic alone. Don't you think it's best to honor Mother Goose's mission by spreading as much hope as we can, even if our method has changed?"

"I guess so." I sighed.

"Don't look so glum! We still preserve our tradition by saving one day each week to distribute wishing cakes the old-fashioned way. Hopefully our future Goose Ladies will do that, too."

We were both quiet for a moment. But inside I felt more desperate than ever to go on a cake delivery.

"So what's up, kiddo?" asked Aunt Doris. "I know you have something on your mind."

I took a deep breath. "Aunt Fancy just told me the most unfair thing! I'm not allowed to help deliver a wishing cake tomorrow! She said it was Old Cone Hat's, I mean, Aunt Esperanza's decision. Would you please talk to her for me? I've just got to go!"

Aunt Doris sighed. "I'm sorry, kiddo. When we decided to bring you here, we vowed that we would keep you safe."

"But I'm going to miss all the fun."

She stared out the window and gave her gum a good, loud crack. "Unfortunately, the Sinister Sisters might have figured out where you are by now. If they catch you, they'd surely seek revenge for what you did to Raveneece."

"I'm not afraid!" I insisted, although my voice wavered.

"Calm down. Take a deep breath." Aunt Doris put an arm around my shoulders. "Maybe Espy needs you here," she said softly. "There's a rhyme from the Old Times I think you should hear:

> "It takes two strands to make a knot
> And two brave hearts to foil a plot
> Both Grand and Grandie, arm in arm
> To keep the Greedy from our farm
> For if the bond between them breaks

There'll be no more of wishing cakes."

I thought about telling Aunt Doris that I knew Aunt Cone Hat was my great-great-great-grandma. But then she'd know I'd been eavesdropping. I didn't want to have to explain about what I'd been doing at the barn. If the Aunts found out I had Raveneece's eye, I'd only get in more trouble.

"I don't think she wants my help," I grumbled. "She hates me."

"She doesn't know you and you don't know her. That's another good reason to stay."

To: Lucy Chang, Alexa Pinkston
Subject: A Day with Old Cone Hat

Her tall cone hat,
What's up with that?

Is that mountain on her bean
The thing that's making her so mean?
Does it sleep with her in bed
Snuggled up atop her head?
Are there spiders under there?
Rats and beetles in her hair?

Her tall cone hat,
What's up with that?

Miss you a lot!
Pixie
P.S. Wish me luck tomorrow—I think I'm going to
need it!

CHAPTER TWENTY-TWO
Ye olde Garrulous Visitor

While everyone else went to deliver wishing cakes, I stayed at the farm with Aunt Esperanza. She kept me working as if I were Cinderella. After I'd cleared the dishes and scrubbed the pans, she said the potager needed attention. I weeded, watered, re-staked tomato, bean, and strawberry plants, picked beetles off the roses, and hoed the rows till they were ruler straight. Being busy made the morning go super fast, though. I was amazed when Aunt Esperanza called, "Lunchtime!"

To be fair, I should say that she'd been working as hard as me. Her rocking chair hadn't seen her bony butt even once all morning. Sometimes I'd catch her watching me. But she never complained about the job I was doing.

I stood up and wiped my hands on my shorts. "I'll just take a peanut butter sandwich out to the meadow," I told her. "I like to eat with Destiny. La Blanca usually comes, too."

"Then we'll picnic together. You can make me a peanut butter sandwich, too. I'll get Destiny and La Blanca."

We sat on a scratchy old horse blanket in the field. "When I was young, I used to think I could eat peanut butter sandwiches every day for the rest of my life," Aunt Cone Hat said. "I actually tried. I ate them for fifty-seven days in a row."

I stopped chewing and looked at her. "Why'd you stop?"

"On the fifty-eighth day, I couldn't even look at the jar."

"How long did you wait before you started eating peanut butter again?"

She held up her sandwich. "This is the first one

I've had since then."

"Really?"

"Really." She took a big bite and burped. Just like Gray!

I couldn't imagine her as a kid. She seemed like one of those people who'd been born a grown-up. I wondered if she'd had friends, told jokes, or jumped in piles of leaves.

We watched Destiny and La Blanca waddle across the grass together. "Did you hatch La Blanca in an incubator?" I asked.

"No, La Blanca was hatched by a chicken. We had a coop in our backyard and I found her in the middle of a bunch of baby chicks."

I grinned. "Kind of like the ugly duckling."

"Oh, no." She shook her head. "La Blanca wasn't ugly a day in her life."

"Neither was Des," I said. "She was the cutest thing ever. She hatched from an egg Gray and I found in our woods. My dad made us an incubator, but we weren't sure if the egg would ever hatch."

Aunt Cone Hat was licking her fingertips. She stopped for a second to say, "You were lucky."

"I know. Don't you think geese make the best pets?"

She smiled. "Yes, I do."

I ran my finger over the fluff of cloud I wore on my pinky. "Um, I was wondering . . . what you think of Dewey?"

"Who's Dewey?"

"The little male gosling with bumblefoot? Gray says he's getting better, but it will be a while before he's all healed up. Maybe we should keep him here at Chuckling Goose."

"We already have our two males, Commander and Alexander, to protect the flock. They made peace with each other a long time ago. I don't think they'd make it easy for a little gosling. He could get hurt."

"I know, but Dewey isn't a fighter. He's sweet. Besides, Gray's been working on getting them to accept him."

"Why don't I go see him when I have some time," said Aunt Cone Hat.

I decided not to tell Gray. I didn't want to get his hopes up.

When we'd finished eating, Aunt Esperanza pushed herself off the blanket. I thought I heard her bones creak. "I have another job for you."

"Okay." I'd been hoping I could write to my friends at home, but her list of chores seemed unending.

"I'd like you to take Thomas for a trot."

"Do you mean ride him?"

"Well, he's not going to ride you," she replied.

"But I've never ridden a horse before."

"Oh, Thomas will teach you. I'd do it myself if my knees weren't bothering me."

We brought Des and Blankie back to the barnyard and headed to the paddock, where Thomas was waiting. Wyatt must have saddled him up earlier. Had Aunt Cone Hat planned this outing for me all along? I felt a happy buzz of possibility inside.

Although Thomas was old, I thought he was beautiful. He had a coat the color of a golden acorn and a dark brown mane that fell on his forehead like cute bangs.

My mysterious secret grandmother showed me how to sit properly in the saddle and how to hold the reins. Thomas walked me around and around the paddock until I thought we'd both get dizzy. Finally he stopped in front of the gate.

"Okay, he thinks you're ready," she said. The latch squeaked as she opened it and let us into the meadow.

Thomas and I headed for the side of the field that was shaded by the deep green hills beyond, the ones

I'd thought about running off to. I was enjoying the way my body kept rhythm with a horse, when I began to think of a poem:

> The back of a horse is like a throne
> It can make you feel the world's your own
> Forget the phone and the TV
> You've hills and trees for company.

The sight of a van bumping along the deserted road that circled the field interrupted my thoughts. There was black with white lettering on its side, though it was too far away for me to read what it said.

Did the Sinister Sisters have a truck?

Without thinking about how to do it, I turned Thomas around. We headed back to the barn at a trot.

I'd just reached the corral when the truck pulled up. I looked around for something to defend myself with and spotted a rake. Then I saw Aunt Cone Hat was sitting at the entrance to the barn on a folding chair. She didn't stand up when the driver, a woman in a black T-shirt that said "Garrie's Grocery," got out of the truck.

"Esperanza! I haven't seen you in ages. You never come into town these days." The driver shook her headful of choppy gray hair and grinned.

Aunt Esperanza rubbed a hip. "My old bones just can't take it anymore, Garrie," she said. I knew that wasn't the truth. She'd spent the morning doing everything I did, and more. She made half a dozen trips up and down her kitchen stepladder every morning.

Garrie squinted at her. "I see you've still got that pyramid on your head," she said. "Or do you call it a baker's hat now?"

"You know darn well what it is," said Aunt Esperanza.

I pressed my lips together so I wouldn't laugh. But then Garrie said, "Doris didn't mention you had a new girl."

"She's just a maid. Doesn't know a thing about baking." Aunt Esperanza flicked a hand at me like she was shooing a gnat. "Bring Thomas into his stall and get him some water," she snapped.

My eyebrows shot up. But she sent me a quick look warning me not to disagree.

"But Espy, you haven't even introduced us!" said Garrie.

Old Cone Hat looked like she'd swallowed something bitter. "Jane Garrulous, meet Trixie."

Trixie! I almost burst out laughing.

"Pleased to meet you, Trixie. You can call me Garrie. Everyone does."

The word *garrulous* had been on one of my vocab tests last year. When I remembered what it meant, I had to cover my smile.

"What are you doing here, Garrie? Didn't you see the sign that says 'Private Road'?"

"I didn't think that was meant for your friends, Espy," answered Garrie. "Besides, I'm doing you a favor. I brought that red felt you ordered. Are you making yourself a new hat?"

"None of your beeswax! And you know Doris could have picked it up for me."

"True. But I also wanted to talk to you about getting more cakes for the store. Lately I've been running out before the end of the week. Some of my best customers have been disappointed. Doris says you're already on baking overload, but I thought as a friend, you might add a few extra cakes to my order."

Aunt Esperanza frowned. "Why do you need more now? We've been selling you the same number of cakes for years."

"I've got new customers! They're in my store every day gobbling slices of cake like starved turkeys. I can't keep up with them!"

Aunt Esperanza's face darkened. "Come, let me show you the potager while we discuss it. I've put in a lot of new plants since you were last here." She slipped an arm through Garrie's and steered her away from me.

"Pixie!" she snapped without turning around. "I told you to take care of Thomas!"

"You mean Trixie," I said in a snarky voice that my mom would have scolded me for. I slid off Thomas and led him away, wondering why she couldn't have asked me nicely.

"See you at the town fair, Trixie," called Garrie.

CHAPTER TWENTY-THREE
ye olde Truth

I was sitting on the gate to Thomas's stall, scratching behind his ear, when Aunt Esperanza found me. "I see you got his saddle off," she said.

"It wasn't hard," I answered, reaching over to scratch Thomas's other ear. "Your friend Garrie seemed nice. Why did you tell her my name's Trixie?"

"Because I'm cautious—something you should be, too! Garrie's harmless, but she's a gossip. We used to be Goose Girls together."

I didn't mention I'd already heard that from Gray.

Old Cone Hat would probably have called him a gossip, too. "Why isn't Garrie a Goose Lady now?" I asked.

"Because she couldn't rhyme to save her life, even though we tried and tried to teach her. She's only distantly related to the family, I guess just too distant to have the gift of rhyme."

"That's sad," I said, trying to sound sympathetic. But my heart clanged like an alarm. Raveneece Greed couldn't rhyme, either.

Aunt Esperanza clucked. "I hate to admit it, but I missed Garrie when she left. Though I used to see her occasionally at the grocery store."

"Why don't you visit her there anymore?"

"What makes you think you can ask!" Aunt Esperanza said sharply.

"I have a right to know!" I exclaimed. "I'm part of this family, too."

There was silence. Thomas snorted. "I was afraid I'd bring trouble to her doorstep."

"Trouble? Do you mean the Sinister Sisters?"

Esperanza nodded. "For a long time, we didn't hear from them. We delivered wishing cakes, sure that ordinary people would get their birthday wishes and that hope would be safe. But unfortunately, they always return."

I swallowed. "H-how many of them were there?"

She shrugged. "It was hard to tell. Only Raveneece came to town, and not very often. But when she could afford it, she would go to Garrie's for flour. Perhaps the sisters made their living selling their worm and beetle cakes to unsuspecting people. The only thing I'm certain of is that they were still trying to make wishing cakes."

"Did any of them ever come here to the farm?" I wasn't sure I really wanted to hear the answer.

"Oh, worse than that! One day Raveneece saw Doris dropping Wyatt and Pip at Garrie's before school. Raveneece sent us a message saying that she was watching those kids. She asked for a wishing cake as payment for *keeping them safe*."

I sucked in my breath. "What did you do?"

"I sent word to Garrie to let me know when Raveneece would be back to pick up her wishing cake. When she arrived, I was waiting." A smile crossed the old Cone Hat's face. "But not with a cake! I showed her what I'd do if she ever bothered Pip or Wyatt."

"What?"

Aunt Esperanza looked at me. "I froze Raveneece," she said quietly. "Though it was just for a few minutes, she never bothered our kids again."

"You have that power, too!" I exclaimed.

I held my breath, waiting for her to declare, *"That's because I'm your great-great-great-grandmother."* But she only nodded and turned away, saying "Come on, let's go back to work."

CHAPTER TWENTY-FOUR
Ye olde Powerful Stories

Aunt Esperanza and I ate leftover mac and cheese for dinner. She seemed far away in her thoughts. Afterward, when I asked to be excused, she seemed glad to let me go. She even said I could use the computer in her office to write home. I guess she'd had more than enough of me.

The office was like a library. There were floor-to-ceiling bookshelves and lamps with good light for reading. On the desk was a photo of Esperanza and La Blanca, when Blankie was just a gosling. It seemed sad that there were no other photos of family. It made me feel guilty about taking my family for granted.

To: Mom and Dad Piper
Subject: Super Sorry!

I'm sorry that I didn't write
I really am okay
I've made new friends, I'm having fun
Still miss you every day!
Love you,
Pixie
P.S. When I get home, I'm cooking you breakfast!

To: Lucy Chang, Alexa Pinkston
Subject: Just Thinking

Have you got granny's sunny smile
And grandpa's love of sport?
When you grow up will you be like
Your mom, a judge in court?

I think I've got my great-gran's moods

And also her green thumb
But I won't wear her pointy hat
I still think it looks dumb

Ha-ha!
Pixie

I'd just pressed Send when I heard the office door creak open. "Time for bed, Pixie. The others won't be back until after midnight."

"Okay," I replied.

"You can take Destiny upstairs, so you won't be lonely."

For a moment I was too shocked to say anything. She was giving me permission to let Destiny into the house! I spun around in my chair to thank her. But my perplexing great-great-great-grandmother was already gone.

On my way down the hall, I noticed the light still on in the dining room. When I peered in, I saw her seated in her chair with her head drooping over the table.

"Good night," I said quietly.

She looked up and nodded. I wondered if her big cone hat was becoming too heavy. "Everyone sleeps in the morning after deliveries," she said. "You don't have to come down tomorrow until eight. It will give us plenty of time to prepare brunch."

But the next morning, I got up early as usual. I had something to do. Destiny snuggled into my pillow while I pulled on shorts and a T-shirt. "Quiet, sweetie," I whispered as I lifted her out of bed. She honked in protest anyway, but not one of the other apprentices stirred.

With Des nestled in my arms, I grabbed my photo of Sammy and tiptoed out of the room. On my way to the kitchen, I stopped in Aunt Cone Hat's office and put the photo beside the one of her and La Blanca. I wrote a note to leave beside it.

"Here is a photo of Sammy, your great-great-great-grandson."

She was already in the kitchen, making muffins when I arrived!

"Good morning," I said as I tied on an apron.

"I said you didn't have to come early," she said, without looking up from the bowl. "But as long as you're here, I need a half-dozen eggs cracked now."

I smiled and hurried to the fridge.

* * *

Later, once everyone was up and seated at the table, it was time for sharing delivery stories.

"Gray and Pip, why don't you begin," said Aunt Doris.

Gray wiped his mouth on his sleeve and took a deep breath. "Okay. The person we were delivering to lived on the fourth floor of an apartment building. No one was home when we rang the bell, so it looked like this was going to be easy. Pip used her power to unlock the door and I was about to sneak in with the cake when this really ferocious dog attacked me!"

"Yeah, a Chihuahua," said Pip, laughing.

"It had sharp teeth!" exclaimed Gray. "I had to back out and close the door before it took a chunk out of my leg."

Pip rolled her eyes. "It would've been a mosquito-sized bite. Anyway, when we got outside again, I used my power to open the kitchen window. I was really proud, because I'd never tried it on anything so high up. But there was no way to climb the wall. Fortunately, Aunt Doris has the power of telekinesis. She used her mind to send the cake through the window."

"You should have seen it, Pix!" exclaimed Gray. "A flying cake!"

It was a little tough to be a good sport, but I nodded and smiled.

Next River bragged about Nell's power to make any noise—the ring of a telephone, a doorbell, a dog's bark, a fire alarm, thunder—anything. "They all sounded real!" he exclaimed. "When we got to the house where our birthday person lived, Nell meowed really loudly. The woman thought she heard a cat crying and hurried to the back door. I tried the front door, but it was locked. I figured I'd have to climb in through a window, but Aunt Fancy said lots of people leave an extra key under the doormat, so I checked. She was right! I delivered the cake through the front before the woman came back. The whole thing took less than three minutes."

"Well, it only took two minutes for me and Winnie to deliver our wishing cake," Rain bragged as if she were competing with her twin. "We stood beneath the kitchen window of the house where our birthday person lived and Winnie sang a few bars of this song called 'Mr. Sandman.' She has a beautiful voice! Instantly the family that lived there put their heads on the table and began to snore. Even the dog fell asleep! I left the cake in the middle of the table and snuck back out, without anyone catching me."

Imagining the family's surprise when they awoke and saw the cake made me laugh. But the best story belonged to Perrin and Wyatt. On their way to deliver their wishing cake, Wyatt—who drove a little too fast around a curve—rolled the car into a ditch on the side of the road.

"The wheels kept turning, but the car was stuck," Wyatt explained. "I was afraid it was going to get dark before we got out of there. But Perrin got us moving again."

"How?" I asked.

"It was nothing," said Perrin with a little shrug. "All I did was lift up the rear end of the car and give it a good push back on the road."

I gaped at Perrin, who didn't look like she even could lift a bowling ball. "What happened after that?" I asked. "Did you deliver a cake?"

"Oh yes. When we finally found the right address, all Wyatt had to do was put on his postman's hat and say 'Special Delivery.' The girl who took the cake inside was so delighted, she didn't even ask who it was from." Perrin shook a fist. "But I told Wyatt the next time he didn't obey the speed limit—*pow!*

I'd deliver him to the moon."

"And she could do it, too!" Wyatt exclaimed. We all laughed.

"Do you want to share something from your day, Pixie?" asked Perrin.

"Um, sure." Suddenly I realized I wasn't jealous of their days at all. "Aunt Esperanza let me ride Thomas yesterday. First we walked around the corral, but then we trotted on the field. It was super fun!"

I looked over at Old Cone Hat, but she was pushing her chair back and didn't act as if she'd heard me.

"Need more coffee," she mumbled. But when she passed behind me on her way to the kitchen, I felt her quick squeeze on my shoulder.

"Wow! That's really cool," said Rain. "I love horses."

"You love armadillos, too," River said.

I smiled. Someday I wanted a delivery story of my own. But I liked yesterday just the way it was.

CHAPTER TWENTY-FIVE
Ye olde Bad News of the Week

While everyone else gathered in the TV room, I helped Aunt Esperanza make popcorn and arrange cookie platters. Finally I went to sit on the rug with Gray, Pip, Rain, and River.

"Welcome to *Good News of the Week*," said Toni Tellsit from the crumbling steps of a long, low building. "This is Crumbleview Elementary School. The students say it's a wonderful place, but over the years it's become overcrowded. There isn't space for a technology center. Science classes are conducted in the cafeteria.

Crumbleview even lost its library a few years ago, when they needed the space for another classroom."

"Holy goose!" exclaimed Pip. "Gray and I delivered our cake to someone in Crumbleview."

"What this school does have," Toni Tellsit continued, "are hardworking, deserving teachers and kids. That's why the good news this week is really great news. Crumbleview Elementary is getting a new addition."

We heard the sound of kids cheering as Toni Tellsit walked down into the schoolyard, where the students and staff were waiting.

"This is Principal Darnell James, who inspires the students every day," Toni Tellsit said.

I liked how the principal looked. His jeans, plaid shirt, and beaming face reminded me of my dad.

"Please tell us the good news, Mr. James," Toni Tellsit said, holding up the microphone.

"Please call me Darn, Toni—everyone does," said Mr. James. "Well, we started by having the students vote on what they thought our school needed most. They were the ones who chose a library. Our idea was to raise money for it as a community. We held bake sales, read-a-thons, and other fund-raisers. Some students donated their weekly allowance or babysitting money. We figured it might take us four or five years to raise enough to start construction. But Cheralyn here helped us get there a lot sooner." The principal gestured to the girl beside him, who looked about my age. She had bright eyes and a messy ponytail. I liked her right away.

Toni Tellsit nodded and smiled. "Could you explain how you helped your school get its library, Cheralyn?"

"Sure. I turned ten on the last day of school. Every year on my birthday, I have a family party with my grandparents, aunts, uncles, and cousins. This year I asked everyone to make donations toward the library. I even made a wish on my birthday cake for enough money to get the library going faster. After I blew out the candles, I began opening the envelopes my family had given me."

Cheralyn's eyes widened as if she were surprised all over again. "Inside my Uncle Orson's envelope, there was a lottery ticket. Oh, and a quarter because it was the scratch-off kind."

"That must have been unexpected," said Toni Tellsit.

"Not exactly. Uncle Orson is my mom's baby brother. She nicknamed him Dreamer when he was still a kid." Cheralyn brushed back a strand of hair.

"Anyway, Uncle Orson insisted I scratch it off right then and there."

"And?"

Cheralyn shook her head like she still couldn't believe what came next. "The ticket was a grand prize winner. Twenty-five thousand dollars!"

"Wahoo!" Toni Tellsit exclaimed. "What did Uncle Orson say?"

Cheralyn shrugged. "Nothing. He fainted."

At first we were laughing so hard we didn't hear the ringing. Then Aunt Bernie shouted, "Hush! I think I heard your office phone, Espy."

Aunt Esperanza launched herself out of the rocking chair and rushed out of the room.

I was thinking about how Cheralyn had donated her birthday money for her school library and whether I'd have done the same, when Aunt Esperanza appeared in the doorway. Her face seemed to have grown more wrinkled in the few minutes she'd been out of the room.

"Rain and River, come with me," she said in a hoarse voice. "Doris, you'd better come, too."

Silently we watched them follow her out of the room. Gray plucked at his shoelaces. I lay my head on my knees. From behind me, Winnie leaned forward and squeezed my shoulder.

CHAPTER TWENTY-SIX
Ye Olde Trouble Finds Its Way

It was agonizing knowing that bad news was waiting for Rain and River. When Aunt Esperanza returned to the TV room, she just stared at us for a long moment. "There's been a fire at United Pets and People," she said finally. "It was started by a lightning strike to the barn, but it spread quickly to the other buildings. Rain and River need to be with their parents. Doris will take them home in the truck tonight."

The air in the room grew so heavy, I felt like I was breathing soup. Life at Chuckling Goose Farm had been like living inside a fairy tale. There were cakes that granted wishes. There were mixing spoons that called batter imps. There were Sinister Sisters who wanted to steal our rhymes. We hadn't been concerned about the ordinary kind of troubles, like sickness, accidents, or fires. We'd almost forgotten those things could happen.

When Aunt Esperanza said my name, I jumped. "Pixie, go upstairs and help Rain. I asked her to pack a small bag to take home with her. We can send the rest of her things later. Wyatt, you get Drizzle from the barn and help River with his things. Everyone else should stay here and give them some time."

I found Rain sitting on her bed, studying a photo. The duffel bag beside her was open, but she hadn't packed yet.

"Rainey—I'm sorry. Aunt Esperanza told us what happened," I said softly, so I wouldn't startle her.

When she looked up, her face was damp and splotchy. "United Pets and People is gone, Pixie. Our house was destroyed, too."

My throat burned with tears as I sat down beside her. She was staring at the photo of her family that had been taken in front of the clinic. Everyone was smiling at the camera. Even the animals seemed to be grinning.

"Are they all okay?" I asked.

Rain nodded. "All except for our three cats. My dad thinks they ran off, and that they'll be back soon."

Footsteps sounded in the hall. Then Pip appeared in the doorway. "Hey, can I come in?" she asked.

Rain nodded, but for a moment Pip just stood there. I was surprised to see a tear running down her cheek. "Cats are quick and clever," she said, wiping her face on her arm. Although I didn't have a cat, I hoped it might be true.

Rain nodded. "My dad says they'll come back. But we're going to live with my grandma until we can rebuild. They're sending Fifi, our pig, and Clover, our goat, to a farm for a while."

"I wanted to give you something before you go." Pip took a jelly jar stuffed with money from her bottom drawer. It was mostly coins with a few bills mixed in. "You might need this," she said, handing it to Rain.

"I can't take your money, Pip."

"Sure you can. You could use it to buy food for the animals," Pip said, placing it in Rain's lap. "Anyway, it's not much. I spent a lot of it on candy at Garrie's Grocery."

"I have some money, too," I suddenly remembered. I took the book I'd brought from home—*Ella Enchanted*—from my nightstand and flipped to the back, where I'd tucked the ten-dollar bill I'd gotten from my mom. "Add this to the jar," I said.

"Thanks, both of you." Rain untied the two red and white woven bracelets she always wore and gave each of us one. "Here, I want you to have these, so you don't forget me."

"We'll wear them until you return," I told her, tying mine on tightly.

"Rain," River was calling from downstairs, "Aunt Doris says we're leaving in five minutes!"

The three of us stuffed pajamas, T's, shorts, and underwear into Rain's duffel bag. When it was full, Pip offered to take it downstairs to River.

"Tell him I'll be down in a sec. I just have to pack my toiletries and find my flip-flops," said Rain.

When Pip was gone, I unwound the soft gray thread I'd been wearing around my pinky since I'd arrived.

"For good luck," I said, twisting it on Rain's pinky.

"Pixie! I can't take this," she protested.

"You have to! You can give it back when you return," I said.

We collected her hairbrush, her toothbrush, her shampoo and conditioner. She found her flip-flops under the bed.

Pip came back just in time for a last good-bye. We gave each other one more hug and Rain ran down the stairs.

"Tell us as soon as you find the cats!" Pip called after her.

CHAPTER TWENTY-SEVEN
Ye olde Story of Pip

After Rain left, Pip punched the mattress. "I hate it when anyone leaves!" she exclaimed.

"Does it happen often?"

"Every August when everyone goes home except Wyatt and me." Pip turned Rain's bracelet around and around on her wrist. That's when I noticed the bruises on the inside of her arm. They were black-and-blue marks about the size of a nickel.

I touched one with a fingertip. "How'd you get these?"

She pulled her arm away. "Just some friends fooling around."

That didn't seem very friendly to me. But I'd been hit in the face with a softball by someone I thought was a friend. Sometimes things were more complicated than they sounded.

"Do you know Wyatt and I have been living here most of our lives?" Pip asked. "Our mother died when I was three days old and our father had to go back to the navy. He knew that he was somehow related to the Goose Ladies—he remembered meeting Aunt Doris once when he was a kid. So when she showed up and said they would take care of us while he was away, our dad was relieved. Then his ship was lost at sea."

My stomach dipped the way it did when my mother talked about losing her parents. "I'm sorry, Pip," I whispered.

She shrugged. "It's okay. When we were little, we were happy enough. But now it's lonely being the only kids around here for most of the year."

I nodded. All I could see out the window were fields and trees. They were beautiful, but there wasn't another house around for miles—which meant there were no neighbors. "Didn't you go to school, though?" I asked.

"At first the aunts tried to homeschool us. But they were really busy baking everyday cakes and wishing cakes. Wyatt got ornery and I cried a lot. They figured out that we needed friends. So they decided to send us to Buttercrunch Elementary and Middle School. When school got out, we used to stay in town until Aunt Doris could pick us up."

I nodded. "At Garrie's Grocery."

Pip's eyebrows rose up. "You know Garrie?"

"She was here last week when everyone was out delivering cakes. Aunt Esperanza didn't seem too happy to see her."

"Well that's no surprise," said Pip, shaking her head. "The Aunts have always been really careful about not being seen in public or letting anyone near Chuckling Goose. That's why they've got those signs on the road that say 'PRIVATE PROPERTY' and 'NO TRESPASSING'! They never even let a school bus come here."

"Taking a school bus is overrated," I said. "Some days it's like riding with a tankful of sharks."

Pip smiled. "When we were little, Aunt Doris would drop us at Garrie's Grocery. It's not far from school, and Doris delivered cakes there anyway. She arranged to give Garrie five extra cakes a week in return for her taking us the rest of the way to school and picking us up. We stayed at the store until Aunt Doris took us home. I didn't mind. I liked helping Garrie dust the cans and restock the shelves."

I wondered if Pip knew the story of how Aunt Esperanza had frozen Raveneece because she'd threatened to harm her and Wyatt. I didn't ask, though. It wasn't mine to tell.

"Now Wyatt and I walk to school on our own," Pip said. "But sometimes he stays late for extra classes or sports, so I still go to Garrie's to wait until he or Aunt Doris can meet me. And every Friday, Garrie actually pays me to help out."

"That's cool," I said.

"Yeah. In the fall, I won't need anyone to come for me. I can get home alone. Wyatt and I figured out a shortcut through the woods. I don't even have to take the road." Suddenly she grabbed my arm. "You can't tell anyone about that—not even Rain."

"Don't worry, I can keep a secret," I assured her. The truth was, I was surprised she'd confided in me. I hadn't always been sure we were friends.

"Hey, can I wear one of your T-shirts tomorrow?" she asked. "I'm almost out of laundry again."

"Sure, you can borrow anything you want," I said. "Anytime."

* * *

During the next week, helping with breakfast, writing new wishing rhymes, baking cakes, taking care of Destiny, and helping Aunt Esperanza with the garden kept me really busy. But at night I thought about Rain and River a lot. I'd written e-mails to Rain, but so far there'd been no answer. I told myself to be patient, which was something I'd never been very good at.

I tried to imagine what the twins were doing. I was lucky. I didn't know how things worked when you lost everything like that. But lately I'd started worrying about it. Where would the Aunts go if Chuckling Goose Farm was destroyed in a fire? And what about Pip and Wyatt, who lived here, too? What would happen to the geese, and Thomas, and the cows? Some nights those thoughts kept me awake past midnight—and the only thing to do was go to the computer. More and more, writing to my friends became like keeping a diary.

To: Rain and River
Subject: My Life in **Nines**
My lunch was peanut butter
Nine times in a row

To tie Aunt Cone Hat's record
I've forty-eight to go

I've loaned my roommate Pippi
T-shirt number **nine**
But each one comes back dirty
And smelling like a swine.

It's been **nine** days since you left us
Though it feels more like a year
I wonder if you found your cats
And if you'll return here.

Miss you 9x9x9x9x9x9x9!!! (4,782,969)
Pixie

CHAPTER TWENTY-EIGHT
Ye olde Mother Goose Rhyme

I was totally surprised at breakfast on Monday when Perrin said, "Today you'll be baking your own wishing cake, Pixie. Aren't you excited?"

I dropped my fork, splattering drops of syrup on my shirt.

"Don't tell me you forgot your birthday's tomorrow," said Gray.

"I didn't forget it; I misplaced it," I replied, dabbing at the mess with my napkin. "I lost track of the days."

"If I was getting a wishing cake, which I'm *not*," said Gray, looking around the table at everyone, "I'd know when my birthday was to the *exact second*." He stuffed a muffin in his mouth and kept on talking. "And by the way, isn't it unfair that Wyatt and I don't get them?"

Pip smirked. "Trying out a wishing cake is part of our *work*, Gray. Anyway, you might get a wishing cake someday. You have as much of a chance as any other random person."

Gray just sighed and shook his head.

I looked at my lap, so he wouldn't see me smiling. I'd been deciding between two wishes—going on a cake delivery or taking a vacation in Hawaii. If I did choose Hawaii, I was planning to include Gray in my wish so he could come along with my family and me. I might do it just to hear him whoop.

After breakfast, I made a quick trip to the barn to see Destiny. Then I rushed back to the kitchen, tied on my apron, and slung Stumpy around my neck. By the time the rest of the apprentices were ready, my patience was gone. I couldn't help hopping from foot to foot while Perrin led the rhyme that began all of our baking sessions:

"Mix and chatter, mix and chatter
That's the way to coax a batter
If a pleasing rhyme you say
Your request it will obey."

Since the birthday cake I'd be making was my own, I got to choose the kind I wanted, and I wanted one with cinnamon. Lots of it! When I told that to Perrin, she snapped her fingers.

"I know just the one—the snickerdoodle! It's a cinnamon and vanilla butter cake with brown sugar and cinnamon buttercream icing."

Yum!

I gathered the ingredients and added them to my bowl one at a time. Then I put Stumpy to work mixing the batter while I placed my hand over my chest. The rhyme I recited seemed to pop right out of my heart:

"Cinnamon is the scent of home
One sniff and I am there
My mom in a costume, my dad in his jeans
And Sammy with food in his hair

"If only every family
Could gather round a cake
Hope would spread across the world

With every wish they make."

I was stirring in slow, wide circles when I saw an ocean in the batter. I was riding on a surfboard with Destiny, surrounded by friendly dolphins. Gray was waving to them from a palm tree he'd climbed to pick coconuts. Sammy was sitting on the beach, making sand cakes with his pail and "feeding" them to Mom and Dad.

I felt like diving right into the bowl!

But in another moment, the scene disappeared and a bubble rose in the center of the batter. When it popped, a face appeared. Straight lines for eyes, small, pouty lips, and swirly cheeks.

"Baw-wing."

"My family is not boring," I snapped.

"Maybee. But yaw poem is."

I tried not to smile. "Gee, thanks," I said.

"Twy again!"

"Don't you ever like a rhyme the first time?" I grumbled, though I was beginning to like this batter imp. It was sounding more and more like Sammy.

"Come on aweady!"

"Hold your horses!" I snapped.

"You mean gooses."

"Geese, not gooses," I said, "and be quiet so I can

concentrate." I squeezed my eyes shut until I came up with another rhyme:

"Pineapple-coconut-upside-down cake
That's what the aunts in Hawaii make
Mix in hope to make it sweet
Wish . . . blow . . . and then you eat!"

"Okay, bedda." There was a pop, and then the face was gone.

I hadn't expected the imp to give in so fast. It hadn't even asked for a tickle. I stirred it gently, hoping to coax it back. Instead, waves of batter splashed against the side of the bowl and sprayed my face. I grabbed a towel to wipe my eyes. When I looked back again, I saw her.

"Mother Goose! I—I wasn't expecting you," I whispered.

"I've composed a birthday rhyme for you, Cinnamon Girl," she replied. In her singsong voice she began to chant:

"Watch out for things that glitter
Not everyone is fair
Trouble comes along in threes
Make sure that you take care!"

"Er, thank you," I said, although her gift sounded more like a birthday warning. "But I don't get it.

What does it mean?"

The eyes in the bowl looked annoyed, as if Mother Goose was getting tired of my questions:

"Diamond, emerald, ruby, beware

Of the sparkly sisters you'll meet at the fair."

"The fair? I—I don't think I'll be going," I stammered. "The Aunts never let me go anywhere."

Suddenly the batter was just batter again.

CHAPTER TWENTY-NINE
Ye olde Surprise Journey

I had trouble falling asleep that night. Of course, I was always excited on the eve of my birthday, but the idea of having a wishing cake of my own was making me as greedy as old King Midas. Although I'd gone to bed with the idea of wishing for permission to go on a cake delivery or taking a trip to Hawaii, my mind couldn't quit thinking of new possibilities—a castle for my family instead of our cramped little cottage; enough money to have a pizza party for my friends every week; or maybe my own book of rhymes in every library, just like Mother Goose.

When I finally fell asleep, it wasn't for very long. Suddenly there were hands pulling me out of bed. I clung to the mattress as if it were a life raft, but they held my feet, lifted me under the armpits, and tied a scarf over my eyes. I was twisting and squirming like a fish on a line, until a voice whispered in my ear. "Stop struggling, Pixie; this is going to be fun." It was Winnie.

So I allowed myself to be carried, limp as a load of laundry. They set me down in the kitchen and removed the blindfold.

I stared into my cousins' merry faces. "What's going on?" I asked. I was breathing hard, but I couldn't really be mad at them.

"It's your birthday—time to start celebrating!" Perrin pointed at the grandfather clock in the corner. It was 12:01.

I rubbed my eyes and yawned. "At home we start birthdays at breakfast."

"Well, you can't start at breakfast, if you want to take a moonlight flight," said Perrin.

I looked out the kitchen window. A big crescent moon hung like a golden swing in the dark sky. "But how?" I asked.

"Ask Nell. It was her idea."

Nell's cheeks flushed. "Well, it begins with baking the naughty biscuits I accidentally invented," she explained, sounding both excited and shy. "We'll need a lot of them, so we've got to hurry."

"I'm going flying with biscuits?"

"Yep," replied Perrin. She clapped her hands. "Everyone get your spoons and bowls ready."

The usual baking ingredients—flour, sugar, salt, and baking powder—were already out on the counter. But there was also frozen butter, buttermilk, and baking soda, which was another kind of rising powder.

Nell gave the instructions. "You have to work really quickly, so the butter doesn't melt before we get them in the oven," she explained. "And when it's time to knead the dough, you have to do it exactly eight times."

"How long do they bake?" I asked.

Nell put a finger to the dimple in her cheek. "About fifteen minutes, I think. But we have to watch them carefully. The moment they begin lifting off the baking pans, we have to remove them. That's the tricky part. We're going to catch them up in this." She patted a crisp, white bedsheet.

There was so much excitement in the kitchen, I

felt as if we all might lift off the floor even without flying biscuits. Still, we took the baking very seriously. Although I was super curious about how the moonlight flight would work, I made myself concentrate on getting the recipe just right.

After kneading the dough exactly eight times, I rolled it out and used a cookie cutter to make circles. We all brought our baking pans to the oven at the same time. We were like synchronized swimmers! We could have been in a baking Olympics!

For fifteen minutes Nell and Pip kept an eye on the window in the oven door, while Winnie, Perrin, and I each held a corner of the bedsheet.

"Look—they're beginning to fly!" exclaimed Pip just as the timer bell went off. "Get ready to catch them!" She pulled down the door and the biscuits flitted out of the oven, bobbing and dipping like a flock of sparrows. Quickly we captured them in the sheet and folded it into a lumpy bundle.

Wyatt, River, and Gray were waiting for us in the meadow. Wyatt tied a thick rope to the end of the biscuit bundle, so it looked like a robber's getaway sack. He tied the other end snugly around my waist. Then he tied a second rope around the bundle and handed it to me.

"Hang onto this. It will make your flight more secure," he said.

My Goose cousins all kept a firm hold on the bundle until I was ready.

"It's a perfect night for a biscuit flight," whispered Nell, gazing up at the sky. "There's even a little breeze to move you along."

"Did you do this on your birthday, too?" I asked her.

"Oh no, I'm not brave like you," said Nell in a quivery voice. "You're our first pilot."

"Um thanks, I think," I said, trying to make a joke of it. "But how do I get down? I mean, the moon is pretty far away."

"It's a flight in the moonlight, not to the moon, silly," said Perrin.

"The biscuits never fly for very long, anyway," Nell added. "After a bit they drift down on their own."

"Now, don't let yourself go higher than you can jump comfortably," advised Winnie. "And if you need our help, call right away."

"You'd better let her go already before the rising powder stops working," said Gray. He gave me a big cheesy grin. "I'll do it if you don't want to."

"Thanks, but no thanks," I told him. I took a deep breath. "Okay, I'm ready.""

"Hold on tight," Wyatt warned.

I nodded, too nervous to speak.

Everyone was quiet as Nell stepped forward. She gazed in my eyes and began to recite:

"Flying biscuits bring delight

To a spirited girl on her birthday night

Beneath a moon that's lantern bright

Take her away on a magical flight!"

All at once the apprentices stepped back and I was jerked up in the air, fast and high. I wasn't just hovering over their heads, I was rising toward the treetops.

"Braver than brave, Pix!" shouted Gray.

"Gee, thanks for the reminder!" I called.

Actually, biscuit-flying felt wonderful! The moon lit a golden path across the sky. A breeze set the leaves on the tree branches waving as I passed. Then a sudden gust of wind blew me faster and higher. I reminded myself that Pip had said the rising powder would wear off soon. But I wasn't ready to come down yet. I was having so much fun.

From far below I heard shouting. It sounded like, *"Maybe . . . math . . . wrong"* and *"Too . . . much . . . rising powder."*

Even then, I laughed. It was all so dreamlike, I

wanted to keep going forever.

"Onward and upward!" I urged the biscuits, as if they were flying reindeer. Then I saw the big clump of trees ahead. I was going to crash. I looked down, but I could no longer see or hear anyone.

At first, I thought I was imagining it. Honking! And the sound of wings beating across the sky. It grew louder and stronger until, finally, I saw two geese flying toward me.

"Destiny! Blankie!" I called as they circled me. Destiny tugged the rope from my hand. I shrieked till I remembered I still had the other rope around my waist to keep me from falling. Next I felt a tug on the leg of my pajama pants as La Blanca dipped down to grab hold of the cuff. Together, the geese guided the biscuit ship back to the meadow and brought it gently to earth.

I lay on the ground and caught my breath while the apprentices and the boys came running across the meadow.

"Oh my goose, Pixie, were you scared?" shouted Nell.

"No, it was the most wonderful birthday trip ever!" I said. "But next time I'd use a little less rising powder."

CHAPTER THIRTY
Ye olde Eleventh Birthday

I guess I'd had a bit too much excitement, because I overslept the next morning. When I finally awoke, the other Goose Girls were gone. Quick as I could, I got dressed and ran downstairs. My nose reported that cinnamon rolls, scrambled eggs, and banana nut muffins were already underway. It made me feel guilty for not getting up to help Aunt Esperanza.

"Shh!" I heard as I ran downstairs. Someone giggled anyway. I hurried into the dining room.

"Happy Birthday!" shouted my Goose family. The

table was set, the food was laid out, and everyone except Aunt Esperanza was there.

I pointed at the feast. "Wow!"

"Aunt Espy made this entire breakfast by herself. She wouldn't let any of us help," said Pip.

"Where is she?" I asked.

When the door to the dining room opened again, I couldn't believe my eyes. Aunt Esperanza marched in with Destiny and La Blanca right behind her. Des hurried over and I picked her up and hugged her. "You'd better behave," I whispered.

"Hail, hail, the gang's all here," chirped Aunt Fancy.

"Come on, open your present already," cried Gray, pointing at a square box sitting beside my plate. It was wrapped in white tissue paper and tied with a big red bow.

I set Destiny on my lap while I untied the ribbon and pulled off the paper. With her bill, Des nudged the lid in an excited way.

"Holy goose!" I exclaimed. Inside was a super-cute red cowgirl hat that I knew would be a perfect fit for Destiny. It was just like the one she'd outgrown.

Honk! Honnnk! she squawked, clamping her bill down on the brim and pulling.

"Hold still, Des!" I put it on her wiggly head and adjusted the toggle so it would stay on her. When I was done, she jumped off my lap and paraded around the table. Everyone clapped, which made her puff out her chest and honk louder.

"She loves it and so do I," I said. "Thank you, everyone!"

"Espy's the one to thank," said Aunt Bernie. "She's been working on it every night for weeks."

"Oh, stop exaggerating, Bern! It wasn't much trouble," Aunt Esperanza objected. She took a piece of toast and buttered it as carefully as if she were doing a science experiment. By now I knew that meant she didn't want our attention.

But I could see how much care she'd taken with the hat. The white whip-stitching around the edges was neat and even. There was also a matching white ribbon circling the crown that looked great against the red felt. My mom made costumes, too, so I could tell a beauty when I saw one.

"Thank you, it's really special . . . Aunt Esperanza," I said. I wanted so badly to call her Grandmother, but I couldn't. I had to wait until she asked me. If she ever would.

She stood up and headed to the kitchen,

murmuring, "Got some work to do."

"Can't you stay a little longer?" I asked, before I could stop myself.

For a moment she rested a soft hand against my cheek. Then she continued on her way.

I helped myself to a light, flaky cinnamon roll. At home on my birthday, Mom always made them for me, too. Suddenly I missed her so sharply it hurt.

"I went out early to pick up the mail," announced Aunt Doris, like some kind of mind reader.

I sat up taller. The mail truck didn't come to Chuckling Goose Farm. Our mail went to a post office box a few towns over. Aunt Doris picked it up about once a week. But we mostly used e-mail to stay in touch with our families, anyway.

Aunt Doris reached for her big black purse and pulled out two envelopes, both for me.

I looked at the one on top. In place of a return address, there was a drawing of an acorn, the symbol for my family's house, Acorn Cottage. I ripped it open. There was a handmade card inside. It said "Happy Eleventh Birthday" on the front, with the number eleven spelled out in dried herbs and flowers from Mom's garden—thyme, rosemary, lemongrass, Sweet William, and violets with heart-shaped faces.

It was the best-smelling card ever. Inside there was a twenty-dollar bill, a red balloon, and a poem written by my mom:

> "Happy eleventh birthday
> We miss you while you're away
> We'd like to send you the moon
> But we can't, so here's a balloon."

I loved my mom, although she definitely could have used some help with her poetry.

At the bottom of the card, Dad had used a hot pink magic marker to draw a heart and write both of our names inside. He wasn't much at art, but my throat got tight anyway. And there were purple crayon scribbles all over the card by Sammy, of course.

"Can we see?" asked Pip.

"Sure." I handed it to her and watched as everyone examined it.

The second envelope was from Rain and River. Inside was a bracelet woven of soft, silvery gray fur and a card, which I read aloud:

> "Happy Birthday, Pixie! I combed my rabbit's hair to get the angora for this bracelet.
> Hope you will think of me when you wear it.
> Love, Rain

P.S. The cats came back!!!"

There was also a message from River.

"Happy Birthday, Pixie! I hope whatever you wish on your cake comes true.

Your friend, River"

Neither twin said anything about returning to Chuckling Goose Farm.

We ate quietly for a few moments. I guess, like me, everyone was thinking about the awful thing that had happened to the twins and their family.

"I have something for you, too," Gray said, breaking the silence. From under the table, he retrieved a birthday crown made of white goose feathers.

"Oh, Gray, it's beautiful, but where did you get the feathers?" I asked.

"All over the place. Geese molt once a year, usually in the spring or early summer. I've been collecting the feathers since I got here." He passed the crown to me and I popped it on my head.

"Say cake!" Aunt Fancy ordered, pointing a camera at my grinning face. "You can send this photo to your family."

After a bit Aunt Doris said, "I saw a sign for the fair when I was in town yesterday. It's in two weeks. We're going to have to step up production of the everyday cakes if we don't want to disappoint this year's fairgoers." She looked around the table.

Perrin turned to me and said, "During the week before the fair, we bake until midnight every night in our pajamas."

I tried not to get too interested. Still, I couldn't help asking, "What's the fair like?"

"Practically everyone in town participates somehow," Nell replied. "And people come from the surrounding towns like ants to a sugar bowl."

"It's the best day of the summer," agreed Winnie. "Musicians play, potters pot, painters paint, knitters knit, and restaurants serve their specialties. My mom is the fair's doctor, in case anyone needs medical attention."

"Yeah, like in case they eat too much ice cream," Pip piped up. "There's always a stand where you can get any kind of sundae you want!"

"Or if they eat too much cake. There's never a crumb left," said Aunt Fancy proudly.

"It sounds like fun." I twisted my new bracelet around on my wrist. "Too bad Rain and River will be missing it." *And me, I thought, though I didn't say so.*

"You never know, kiddo," said Aunt Doris.

CHAPTER THIRTY-ONE
Ye olde Decision

The most exciting part of my birthday happened
that night. Seeing my Goose family's faces glowing
in the light of the candles on my wishing cake gave
me a warm feeling. Sure, I'd been calling them aunts
and cousins. But until now those had been words,
not bonds. I wasn't sure when it happened, but I'd
become one of them. I guess it was the small, daily
things that made them feel like family—Pip helping
herself to my T's and socks, Aunt Cone Hat warbling
"Climb Ev'ry Mountain" in the kitchen, Nell sniffling

at everything, Winnie's fortune cookie wisdom, and Perrin bossing everyone around so sweetly no one noticed it.

Like Aunt Esperanza and me, most of my Goose cousins seemed to have awful singing voices, so awful that when they sang "Happy Birthday," we all kept our hands over our ears.

"Hurry up and make your wish before candle wax drips on the cake!" Gray squawked.

"Be patient," Perrin scolded. "It's an important moment."

But I was still undecided! Last night I'd been trying to choose between the Hawaiian vacation or a cake delivery. And now that I'd heard about the town fair, I wanted to go there, too.

Winnie patted my back. "Making a wish is like jumping into a pool, Pixie. When you first hit the water, it feels like a mistake. But as soon as you begin swimming, you know you did the right thing."

"Okay." I squeezed my eyes shut and took the plunge.

"I wish for United Pets and People to get rebuilt as soon as possible!" I said in my head. For good measure I repeated it once more: *"I wish for United Pets and People to get rebuilt as soon as possible!"*

I guess sometimes you don't even know what's in your heart. For a moment my wish had been as shocking as cold water, but as soon as I got used to it, I knew it was right. There was a lot of truth in Winnie's proverb.

I looked up, grinned, and blew out the candles. "It's done!" I announced. "Now let's eat the cake."

For the rest of the week as I did my chores, I thought about Rain. If my wish had worked, her family would be getting a new home for United Pets and People. I couldn't wait till she and River came back to Chuckling Goose. I wanted them to see Destiny in her new cowgirl hat and taste my snickerdoodle cake. (I'd saved slices for them in our freezer.) I wondered if Thomas would let Rain and me ride him together.

On Friday night I was super excited to watch *Good News of the Week*. I couldn't wait to see the reactions of the apprentices and the Aunts when they saw the twins at their newly built home and clinic. I wondered if they would guess it had been my wish that made it happen. But I was never going to admit it. I didn't want Rain and River feeling uncomfortable that I'd used my wish on them.

The after-dinner cleanup felt like it took forever. When we were finally done, I rushed Gray and Pip into the TV room.

"What's your hurry? Don't you want to go see Destiny first?" Gray asked.

"We'll have more time after the show," I replied. "Anyway, it's late. I don't want to miss a minute of Toni Tellsit."

"Oh, Toni Tellsit!" Pip rolled her eyes. "That woman thinks everything is amazing, whether it's a celebrity look-alike pickle or a silly uncle's lucky lottery ticket."

"Come on, you know you love the show," Gray teased, elbowing her.

"Not as much as you!" Pip grabbed a pillow off the sofa and bopped him with it.

It felt as if the other apprentices and the aunts drifted into the room more slowly than usual. Wyatt picked up the remote control and pretended it was a light saber. He wielded it at us, making us laugh, until everyone had arrived.

"Happy Friday and welcome to *Good News of the Week*," said Toni Tellsit, finally. She was wearing pink earmuffs, a puffy white coat, and pink boots. "In case you're wondering, I'm not on a glacier in Alaska or a mountaintop in Switzerland. This week's good news comes from our friends in the town of Dandelion, where, as you can see, I'm standing in a backyard full of snow. And the temperature, dear viewers, is seventy-five degrees."

"Oh! My cousin Ernie lives in Dandelion," said Nell. "This makes me miss him."

"How could this have possibly happened?" asked Toni asked, pointing at the fluffy white stuff at her feet. "Let's ask these incredible children."

Three grinning kids wearing snow boots waved their mittened hands.

"Meet the Smartini kids—Ian, age eleven; Maggie, age nine; and Noah, age five," Toni Tellsit said. "Now which one of you is responsible for making it snow in July?"

"Me!" said Noah, reaching for the microphone. "I wish for a snowy birthday every year—and this time I got one!"

"Well, Happy Birthday," said Toni Tellsit.

"I didn't really believe it would happen," Noah continued. "But Ian said not to give up hope. Then this morning he woke me up and said to look out the window. The snow was covering our lawn, but no place else. It snowed just for me!"

It was true. The other lawns on the Smartinis' block were green and had flowers growing. The neighbors, who were wearing shorts and T-shirts, were mowing or watering their lawns.

"Ian, would you tell us how you were able to make Noah's birthday dream come true?" asked Toni Tellsit.

"Sure. I looked up how to create snow on the Internet. There were all these videos of kids making it in mixing bowls and cake pans. I copied down the recipe. All it takes is baking soda and hair conditioner."

"You girls better not try that with my cake pans," Aunt Esperanza grumbled.

Aunt Doris cracked her gum. "Oh, Espy!"

Toni Tellsit squatted beside Noah. "So you knew this wasn't real snow, right?"

"It is real, it's just different," said Noah. *Splat!* He threw a snowball at the camera.

"Thank you for the demonstration, Noah," said Toni Tellsit, sounding very unthankful. "But kids, if that recipe only makes a bowlful, how did you get enough to cover your lawn?"

"We asked everybody in the neighborhood to make

some," said Maggie. "Plus our grandmas, grandpas, aunts, uncles, cousins, and all of our friends. I made a flyer that told everyone why we needed snow and included the recipe. Our mom made copies for us."

"But how did you get the lawn covered without Noah seeing it?" asked Toni Tellsit.

"That's what I want to know, too," Gray whispered.

Ian chuckled. "That was the most amazing part. Last night after Noah went to bed, everyone who'd made a bowl of snow brought it over. You should've seen the line outside our door! Maggie and I dumped the snow over the lawn."

"It's a good thing we've got a small front yard," Maggie added. "There was just enough to get it covered."

"That is so-o-o great!" exclaimed Pip. "I want to try it."

"Me, too," said Gray.

"Not on my lawn. And not in my mixing bowls," Aunt Esperanza grumbled. But even the other Aunts were chuckling.

The show ended with Noah's family and friends singing "Happy Birthday" and having a big snowball fight. I was glad for Noah, but next week I hoped the good news would be about the rebuilding of United Pets and People.

CHAPTER THIRTY-TWO
Ye olde Hair in the Air

Usually after *Good News of the Week*, we apprentices went to our dorm to hang out before bed. But tonight Pip went running off to the barn with Gray and Wyatt, probably to try making snow. They'd asked me to come with them, but I really wanted to write to Rain.

Aunt Doris caught my elbow. "Hey, kiddo, would you come with me for a few minutes?"

"Um, sure," I agreed.

If Rain had been here, she would have sent me a

look that meant "what's up?" And I would have sent her a shrug and signed TTYL with my fingers. The older girls were so busy chatting about their plans for the fair, they hadn't noticed I wasn't behind them.

Aunt Doris didn't say anything until we were in her room with the door closed. It made me wonder if my birthday was going to end with a big bummer. I must've looked worried, because she said, "Quit worrying! This is going to be fun. We're going to choose a disguise for you to wear to the fair."

"*The fair?*" I rolled my eyes. "Aunt Esperanza will never let me go!"

She sent me a crooked smile. "I've already gotten her to agree to it. Happy Birthday, kiddo!"

I threw my arms around her. "It's the best present in the world! But how did you do it?"

"By assuring her I'd change your appearance so no Sinister Sister would recognize you," Aunt Doris replied.

"But the only one who's seen me is Raveneece."

Aunt Doris tugged lightly on one of my curls. "She might have told the others about this hair of yours," she said, letting it boing back.

I thought for a moment. "Do you really think any of them will come to the fair?"

She puckered her lips—it was the same serious expression my mom sometimes had. "Raveneece may be gone, but I doubt the Sinister Sisters will ever give up on getting a wishing cake. They're wary of our power, but they might try to hide themselves in a crowd of fairgoers."

I looked into the mirror on the wall across from the bed and screwed up my face.

Aunt Doris laughed. "You've still got to be careful, kiddo," she warned. "They might send out some snoops. Garrie told me about three cake-crazy girls who've become regulars at her store. She said they were named for gems, but she couldn't remember which ones."

Gems made me remember Mother Goose's warning.

"Diamond, emerald, ruby, beware
Of the sparkly sisters you'll meet at the fair."

I tried never to think about the terrible moment when I'd shattered Raveneece to pieces. But now I couldn't keep the dark memory away. "I probably shouldn't go to the fair," I said.

Aunt Doris patted my shoulder. "I've given this a lot of thought. I don't want you to spend your life being afraid of the Sinister Sisters. Besides, after what happened to Raveneece, they're probably plenty scared of you. As long as we take precautions, you'll be fine."

I really, really wanted to go. But there was something else. "What about Aunt Esperanza? She's not going. You're the one who told me she shouldn't be alone." I repeated the lines she'd once recited to me:

"It takes two strands to make a knot
And two brave hearts to foil a plot
Both Grand and Grandie, arm in arm
Will keep the Greedy from our farm
For if the bond between them breaks
There'll be no more of wishing cakes."

Aunt Doris smiled. "I'll stay with her. I've already been to plenty of fairs."

My heart began to beat a little faster. I wasn't sure I wanted to go to the fair without Aunt Doris. But I also knew she was right; I didn't want to keep being afraid.

"Why can't one of the other aunts or apprentices stay with Aunt Esperanza?" I asked.

"Espy is the oldest, but the other aunts aren't that far behind her, kiddo," Aunt Doris explained. "Their minds are sharp, but their powers may be rusty. Once Aunt Fancy could lasso a person faster than a cowboy at a rodeo."

I laughed as I pictured it. "Really?"

"Yep. And Aunt Bernie could make people sweat just by staring at them. But they haven't done those things in a while. As the youngest Aunt, it's my responsibility to protect Espy."

"We could both stay here with her," I offered.

"No. You should go, kiddo. If it were necessary, you'd be able to protect yourself and the other apprentices. You could stop things."

"Aunt Esperanza told me she can do that, too—freeze things, I mean."

"Espy hasn't done it for a long time. She's out of practice. We don't know whether she can freeze a flea or a person anymore."

"She doesn't want to do it," I murmured. "And neither do I."

Aunt Doris nodded. "Good. It's right that those who have the greatest power should be the most reluctant to use it. Now let's find a disguise for you. Sit down." She pointed to her bed.

Aunt Doris turned and faced the door of her big cupboard. After a moment she began to chant:

"Hair that's curly, hair that's shiny,
Silky-smooth or tangled
Red, black, brown, blond, silver gray,

Old-fashioned or newfangled
Knotty, frizzy, messy, clean
Long hair, short, or in between
Hair you haven't grown yourself
Will now come floating off the shelf!"

Slowly the cupboard doors began to open and a bevy of wigs came flying out like a flock of colorful, hairy birds.

"Look in the mirror!" Aunt Doris exclaimed.

The wigs were slowly circling above my head.

"Straight blond first," Aunt Doris ordered.

In the mirror I saw a wig that was like Perrin's hair descend onto my head. It felt like a bird getting comfy as it settled itself. I reached up and stroked the pale golden curtain that framed my face. Unfortunately, I didn't look like Perrin. I looked like a broom with eyes, a nose, and a mouth. I frowned.

Aunt Doris cracked her gum as though she agreed with me. "Brown bob next," she called.

In the mirror I saw the blond wig lift off and return to orbit. Then, *plop!* The shiny brown bob landed heavily on my head. I kind of looked like Darth Vader's kid sister.

Aunt Doris and I locked eyes in the mirror and we both shook our heads no.

"Um, I'd like to try on that long black-haired one," I said, thinking of Sage Green, the most popular girl in my fifth grade class. I'd always envied her hair.

Aunt Doris nodded. The helmet hair buzzed off and the black wig fluttered gracefully down.

I turned my head back and forth, making it swing across my shoulders. I ran my hand through the long strands and let them trickle through my fingers. I tucked it behind an ear. I didn't look like a broom or Darth Vader, but I didn't look like Sage, either.

"These freckles ruin everything!" I grumbled, putting my hands to my cheeks.

"Oh, kiddo!" exclaimed Aunt Doris. "What would a Dalmatian be without its spots? Or a fawn, or a ladybug without theirs? Your freckles are part of your charm! However, they *are* very distinctive. We'll have to cover them with makeup, just in case."

I walked toward the mirror, twirling a strand of black hair. I couldn't help grinning at myself.

Aunt Doris was watching me. "Are you sure you don't want to try on the silver wig or the blue one?" she asked.

"No thanks, this one is good," I replied.

She snapped her fingers and the rest of the circling wigs flew back into the cupboard.

"No cinnamon mop, no freckles, no worries," I told myself.

Yeah, right.

CHAPTER THIRTY-THREE
Ye olde Precautions

We baked everyday cakes right up until the last day before the fair. There were thirty-six in all, but Aunt Fancy still didn't think we'd have enough. The Goose Ladies' cakes were always super popular and they always ran out.

At dinner Gray and I listened to the others discuss the things they most wanted to do at the fair. Winnie, Nell, and Perrin liked to buy earrings and bracelets at the craft booths. Pip wanted to eat a double ice cream sundae. Wyatt was thinking of entering the horseshoe toss or the chess competition. The Aunts chatted about seeing old friends.

After we'd cleaned up, Aunt Doris announced, "Early bedtime tonight! We'll have to leave before dawn to set up our booth and tables."

I dawdled in the kitchen, scrubbing the sink until everyone else had left. Then I carried the stepstool to the cupboard where the old yellow sugar bowl was stored. I hadn't checked it in a while and I was afraid someone might have found it.

But it was still there. I glanced quickly over my shoulder before lifting the lid and scraping the crusty sugar with a finger. When I touched the shard that had been Ravenceee's eye, I shuddered. But I made myself dig it out and shove it into the pocket of my jeans.

"Pixie, I thought you were already upstairs," said Aunt Esperanza, surprising me. "What are you doing with that sugar bowl?"

"I saw an ant in the cupboard when I put the berry bowl away this morning," I said, backing down the stool. "I thought I should empty this old sugar out."

She eyed me as if she knew I was up to something. But she only said, "I'd forgotten all about that old crock. Clean it out and we can give it away."

"Okay. I'm too excited about the fair to go to sleep now, anyway."

"Actually, I'd like to talk to you about that."

Carefully I set the sugar bowl on the counter. I wondered if she'd changed her mind and whether I would care.

"I know what it's like to be young and want to have fun," she said.

Really? I wondered. She didn't seem to have much fun these days. "My mom believes everyone should have fun every day no matter how old they are," I said, carefully.

She pulled out a stool and sighed as she sat. "You mustn't let having fun get in the way of being careful tomorrow. Because—"

"I won't!" I interrupted. "Aunt Doris is fixing me up so no one will recognize me. But I promise I'll be really careful anyway."

"Good. I just don't want anything to happen to my . . . to my great-great-great-granddaughter."

For once I was speechless. I knew, of course, but I never thought I'd hear her say it.

"Well? Don't you have any questions?" she asked.

I swallowed. "Why didn't you tell me before? And . . . and why didn't you want me to come here?"

"Because if something happens to you, everyone at Chuckling Goose will be weepy and useless. It will interfere with our mission." She pushed her stool away from the counter and stood. "And because I don't want to lose the best helper I've ever had. Now, go to bed."

"Yes, Grandmother," I whispered.

"Don't call me that!"

"Why?" I couldn't help it—tears stung my eyes.

"Because," she continued more quietly, "it's too dangerous if the word gets out that you're mine. I don't want to lose you, Pixie."

"Okay," I whispered. "Good night."

"Good night." With her leathery old lips, she kissed me on the forehead.

CHAPTER THIRTY-FOUR
Ye olde Fair Day

Before sunrise we huddled together in the back of Aunt Doris's truck—Perrin, Nell, Winnie, Pip, and me, *Trixie*, which was what I'd asked everyone to call me. We were surrounded by stacks and stacks of cake boxes. Although Aunt Doris was driving more slowly than I could walk, it seemed liked magic that they didn't topple over. I tried not to think about Grandie, which was my new secret name for my great-great-great-grandmother. She'd left a hearty breakfast on the table, but hadn't come to the dining room to say good-bye to us.

In her trusty old car, Aunt Bernie drove Aunt Fancy, Wyatt, and Gray—and more cakes. She honked as she passed us and we all laughed.

My Goose Girl cousins had made a fuss over how glamorous I looked in my wig and makeup. But I didn't like the sensation of the wind whipping the long, fake hair across my face or the way my make-up-smeared cheeks felt stiff as a statue's. Maybe I was just feeling nervous.

The town of Buttercrunch was only a short distance from Chuckling Goose. It wasn't very big. Pip pointed out Garrie's Grocery, which was smaller than I'd imagined. We also passed Pip's school, a shoe shop, a hardware supply place, and a bookstore. I didn't get to see much more before Aunt Doris drove onto the fair's parking field and helped us unload the cakes. "I'm going back to Chuckling Goose now," she said. "Be good, be careful, and have fun!"

Lots of people were already heading down the street to the village green. A banner hung across the entrance announcing, "Buttercrunch Town Fair Today!" I spotted Gray and Wyatt finishing our booth—a three-sided shed made of two-by-fours, with a canvas canopy for a roof.

"Hey!" I said, setting my boxes on the long wooden table that served as a counter.

Gray looked right at me, then looked away, confused.

"Heh, heh, heh! I am Treeexie! It's nice to meeet you," I said in my best vampire voice.

His eyes bugged out. "Pix? You, er, kinda look like a vampire . . . pale, pasty skin, black hair—all you need are fangs!"

"Ha! I can't believe you didn't recognize me," I exclaimed. "It's great!"

"Uh, yeah, I guess," said Gray. "Just don't bite anyone."

We high-fived each other and went off to our assigned jobs, Gray helping Wyatt put up tables where customers could sit and eat and me slicing cakes with the other apprentices.

Perrin had just finished writing the names of all our offerings on the menu board when the fair opened officially. It was only 9:00 a.m., but the line at our booth grew fast.

"I wait all year for this day," said a man with an impressive belly. "I'll take a piece of each."

"What's snickerpoodle cake?" a kid wearing very dirty eyeglasses asked, reading the menu. He looked a little disappointed when Perrin told him it was snickerdoodle, not poodle.

The next customer in line was a girl who poked her head across the counter to gape at me. "Pixie?"

"NO, I'm Trixie," I said quickly. Then I blinked. "Rain! I can't believe you're here!"

We both squealed. I ran around the counter and hugged her. Then I pulled her behind the booth. "How'd you recognize me?"

"You forgot to cover up the freckles on your arms and your knees." She stared as if she still couldn't believe her eyes. "Why do you look like that?"

"The Aunts are afraid I'll be recognized by the Sinister Sisters."

Rain's mouth dropped open. "Are they coming here?"

"You know how cautious the Aunts are." I shrugged. "Come on and say hi."

When the rest of the apprentices saw Rain, they crowded around her.

"Excuse me! Who's serving cake?" asked a woman with four little kids.

"We are," said Aunt Bernie. She and Aunt Fancy hurried to help the customers.

"You girls can take a break before the real crowds

start forming," Aunt Fancy said, which was awfully nice, "as long as Rain saves some hugs for us."

We went to sit under a butternut tree. Everyone wanted to know how Rain had gotten to the fair, what was happening with United Pets and People, and whether she was back to stay.

"The most amazing thing happened," she said. "My parents, River, and I were cleaning up the property where United Pets and People used to be. An old rosebush that Mom loved was still alive and she asked us to dig it up, so we could replant it in our grandma's yard."

River appeared then with Gray and Wyatt. River let all of us hug him, although he looked as embarrassed as if he'd been caught kissing a pig.

"Sit down, guys!" shouted Pip. "We were about to hear 'the most amazing thing.'"

Rain shot her twin a grin before she continued. "Both River and I were really upset about how messed up everything was after the fire. Not even the doghouse survived! We were so angry our shovels were practically flying. We hit rocks and dug those up. We found an old stump, some bones our dogs had buried, and more rocks. Then we reached the rosebush's roots. They were so thick and tangled, we felt as if we were battling a nest of snakes. But we finally got that stubborn bush free, and guess what?"

"There was this wooden chest underneath it, about the size of a shoe box," River burst out before anyone could guess. "It was filled with old moldy money!"

My heart started to thump.

"How much money?" asked Gray. "Enough to rebuild United Pets and People?" I think we were all wondering the same thing.

"One hundred and forty-three dollars," River replied. "We tried to give it to Dad. Instead he told us to see if one of Mom's patients, Ms. Finnegan, could use the money. She'd been out of work since she tripped over Inky, her cat, and broke her ankle. Inky's paw was injured, too."

One hundred and forty-three dollars? My wishing cake had been a flop!

"Ms. Finnegan wouldn't take the box of money," said Rain, "but she asked us if we could go to the pharmacy for her meds and the hardware store for light bulbs. She said the reason she'd tripped over Inky in the first place was because the light in the kitchen was out. So first we went to the pharmacy. River paid with the old dollars, which I guess were pretty noticeable, because another customer asked where he'd gotten them.

"After we explained, the man said, 'So you're the kids from United Pets and People! I felt real bad when I heard about the fire at your place and I'd like to help you. I drive a power shovel and I'd be glad to come over and help your folks clear away the debris on your property. Give me the number where you're staying, and I'll call them when I get home.'"

Hmm. So maybe my wishing cake had helped a little, after all.

"Our next stop was Big Pet Supply," River continued. "We wanted to get Inky a bed to rest in and a new toy mouse. While we were waiting on line for the cashier, the woman behind us asked why we were carrying our money in a box. *Because it feels lucky,* I answered. I told her the story of how we'd found it and how the customer in the pharmacy had offered to help us clear the land. And guess what? She was an architect! She said she'd be glad to help Mom and Dad create plans for a place as special as United P and P."

Pip, Wyatt, Winnie, and Perrin whooped. Nell cried, of course.

"Please hold your applause till I'm done," said

River, laughing. "Then we stopped in the hardware store for light bulbs and met a builder." He grinned at all of us. "I think you guys can guess what happened next."

We could!

I'd never been happier to be a Goose Girl.

CHAPTER THIRTY-FIVE
Ye olde Fiendish Friends

After we'd worked a shift in the booth, Aunt Bernie
allowed Rain, Pip, and I to walk around the fair.
That's when we found out Rain's other big news. She
and River were back for the rest of the summer!

"I want to celebrate by treating you guys to ice
cream sundaes," said Pip, pulling us toward a six-foot
tall ice cream extravaganza made of papier-mâché
that stood beside the Sundae Dreams stand. "Pixie,
could I borrow some money?"

She wanted to treat us with my money? Hah!

Then I remembered the jar she'd pressed into Rain's hands. It had been full of bills and coins. I'd given Rain my money, too, but now I had birthday money from Mom.

"I'd be happy to treat," I said. "You don't have to pay me back, Pip."

We waited in line for a long time, but it was worth it. After one cool, sweet bite of my mint chip sundae, I didn't even mind that Pip had dripped strawberry ice cream on the white T-shirt she'd borrowed from me this morning.

We strolled around the fair while we ate. At the Busy Bee stand, I bought Grandie a jar of her favorite, Tupelo honey. And at a booth called Smell the Flowers, I got a lavender sachet that Aunt Doris could hang from her truck's rearview mirror. We stopped under a rainbow canopy to watch a woman make beautiful threads on an old-fashioned spinning wheel. Rain selected a bunch for us to make each other new bracelets.

For a while we listened to a man play the small, handmade musical instruments he'd made. I spent the rest of my money on three bamboo flutes and we tried blowing "Mary Had a Little Lamb" as we returned to Everyday Cakes. It came out sounding more like "Mary Had a Big Screeching Cat."

Back at our booth, Aunt Doris was cleaning crumbs off the counter. "You're not supposed to be here!" I exclaimed. "I thought you were staying with Gr—I mean, Aunt Esperanza."

Aunt Doris shook her head. "Poor Espy spent all morning worrying about you. So I finally agreed to come back here in case you needed me."

I almost wished Old Cone Hat still hated me. "Do you think I should go back to Chuckling Goose now?" I asked.

"No, Espy would be angry if she knew I'd told you she'd been anxious. But for the rest of the afternoon, I'd like you to stay at our booth. Business is finally slowing down, anyway. Perrin, Nell, and Winnie went off to check out the craft stands. If you think you three can handle things, Bernie, Fancy, and I will visit with some of our old friends before it's time to pack up. We won't go far."

For a while we didn't have any customers. I think the heat had finally sent fairgoers looking for shade and rest. Rain, Pip, and I tried playing "Mary Had a Little Lamb" a few more times, but we couldn't get through it without screeching with laughter.

"Looks like we might finally have some takers," said Rain as three girls headed toward us.

"Ugh," Pip moaned. "It's so hot. I don't feel very well."

She did seem awfully pale. "The Aunts have a jug of ice water inside the booth. Maybe you should have a drink and lie down in there for a while," I suggested.

Pip pressed a hand against her forehead. "Okay." She moaned again and backed under the canopy.

The three girls we'd seen stopped to whisper to one another. They were so skinny, they looked like they could use some cake.

"Come on over," I called. "We've still got a few slices left."

The girls studied me for a moment before they walked up to the counter.

"Hi, can I take your order?" I asked.

"Duh," said the shortest and skinniest, waving her fingers in my face. They looked like they could use some soap and water.

"Shut up, Precious Ruby!" the tallest one snapped. "We came to say hello to our friend, Pip." I couldn't tell if her hair was dirty blond or just dirty, but her ponytail was pulled so tight, it made her face look lizard-like.

"Well, I came for cake, not friendship," announced the middle girl, swiping a fingertip over the last piece of chocolate cake. She stuck it into her mouth, which was as wide as a sock puppet's. When she did, I noticed a dark, circular bruise on the inside of her arm. It was like the ones I'd seen on Pip.

"Mind your manners, Precious Emerald," Diamond snapped, "or you'll get a nickel."

I swallowed hard, remembering the rhyme Mother Goose had told me.

Diamond, emerald, ruby, beware!

Of the sparkly sisters you'll meet at the fair!

"Pip's not feeling very well," I said.

"I'm sure she'll feel better when she sees us," said Diamond, smirking at me. "Hey Pip!" she yelled.

Pip looked as if she were in pain as she dragged herself to the counter. "Hi," she said in a flat voice. She and Precious Diamond, the lizard girl, stared at each other, and not in a friendly way.

"Um, do you go to school here?" I asked.

"We're just visiting," said Diamond. "Our aunt brought us."

"So how did you know Pip?"

"None of your business, nosey pants!"

"My name is Trixie," I said.

"Who cares?" Princess Ruby whined. "I want cake now!"

"Sure, I'll get you a piece," I offered.

"Not you, I want Pixie to get it." Ruby poked a finger at Rain.

Rain and I exchanged glances. I'd forgotten I was wearing a disguise. With her red hair and freckles, I guess Rain looked more like me than me.

"How did you know Pixie's name?" I asked.

"Our aunt told us what she looks like." Diamond smirked at Rain. "Hair like rusty springs and skin like oatmeal with raisins."

"Precious Diamond, that's rude!" scolded Emerald.

"Shut your trap, Precious Emerald! She knows I was just joking. Right, Pixie?"

"Um, sure," said Rain. She slid a slice of angel food cake across the table.

"I wanted snickerdoodle!" Ruby cried.

"Sorry, we're out of it," Rain told her. "We're out of practically everything."

"Oops, you earned a nickel!" Ruby pinched the underside of Rain's arm.

"Ouch!" Rain squealed.

"Hey, leave her alone!" I yelled.

Diamond smirked. "Oh, boo-hoo, poor Pixie!

Our aunt told us you were tough, but I guess she was wrong." She thumped her fist on the counter. "Hurry up and get me a slice of caramel crunch cake."

"And a marshmallow fluff cake for me," Emerald added.

Rain bit her lip and pushed two more plates across the counter.

"That will be three dollars," said Pip hoarsely. She was in charge of our two money jars, one for bills and one for coins.

"We're not finished, *friend*," Diamond sneered. "We want three more slices."

"You must really love cake," I said.

"Our aunt said to eat all we want, as long as we keep Pixie busy," Ruby mumbled as crumbs fell from her mouth.

"Precious Ruby, shut your cake hole!" ordered Diamond.

"Diamond, Emerald, and Ruby—you're all named after jewels," said Rain, filling their plates again.

"That's right, and our names all rhyme," said Precious Emerald proudly.

Rain squinted. "Diamond, Ruby, and Pearl?"

"No! *Precious* rhymes with *Precious* and *Precious*, you

dumbette!" sneered Precious Diamond. "Our aunt told us."

Underneath my black wig, I could feel my real hair twisting and curling like angry snakes. Sweat began sliding down my face, dripping makeup into my eyes. There was only one person I knew who really couldn't rhyme, but the last time I'd seen her she'd been shattered into little pieces on the floor of her horrible underground cave.

"I may have something that belongs to your aunt," I said, fighting to keep my voice steady. Carefully, I eased the hard, sharp piece that had once been Raveneece's eye out of my pocket. "Do you recognize this?"

CHAPTER THIRTY-SIX
Ye olde Messengers

I waved the eye under their noses. The three
Preciouses grabbed for it at once.

"I want it!"

"Give it to me!"

"No, me!"

"Finders keepers," I said, holding it up like a powerful charm. "Be careful or this could happen to
you."

"Oh, I don't think we have anything to worry
about. Our aunt has something of yours, too."
Precious Diamond and her sisters began cackling

like a coop of crazy chickens. "You'll be begging for *us* to trade with you very soon."

I felt a curl spring onto my forehead. Makeup dripped off my nose. Not very long ago, Raveneece had stolen Destiny. It was one of the worst times of my life.

Suddenly I realized the Preciouses had stopped laughing.

"You . . . you're getting cinnamon hair and freckles," Precious Ruby said, pointing at my face. "You're starting to look like Pixie." She looked back and forth between Rain and me.

Braver than brave, I told myself. I pulled off my wig, flung it on the counter and shouted:

"I'm the *real* Pixie Piper,
So you'd better watch out
Or I'll freeze your faces
In a permanent pout

"Tell your aunt to desist
Or when cake you eat
Your tongues will shrivel
So *nothing* tastes sweet."

"Nothing? Not even cake? Ever again?" cried Precious Ruby.

"Never, ever again," I answered.

"Our aunt didn't tell us you could do that," said Emerald. But all three sisters began backing away.

"Wait a minute! If you're Pixie Piper, then who's she?" Precious Diamond pointed at Rain.

"None of your busin—"

Rain interrupted me. "I'm Rain, and if you don't get going, I'll send my friends Thunder and Lightning after you." Her voice was eerily quiet, like the calm before a storm.

Emerald and Ruby turned to go. But Diamond cracked a smile. "You should be more careful about choosing your friends, Rain. Being one of Pixie's can be dangerous."

I grabbed Rain's hand.

"Come on, sisters, let's go!" Diamond ordered.

"Wait, you haven't paid," said Pip.

"You're the ones who are going to pay," yelled Precious Diamond. But she and her sisters were already running.

For a moment Pip, Rain, and I were speechless. Although the strange girls were gone, I think we all felt as if our trouble was just beginning.

"I can't believe they're your friends, Pip," I said finally.

"It's not like I had a lot of kids to choose from,"

she grumbled. "Besides, they're not as bad as they sound."

"Oh yeah?" I grabbed her wrist and turned her arm over. "Aren't they the ones who gave you these *nickels*?"

Pip yanked her arm back. "It's just their way of kidding around."

"Yeah, ha-ha," I muttered.

"Hey, what's that?" exclaimed Rain.

I looked up and saw something strange coming across the village green. Was it running or flying? I couldn't take my eyes off it.

As it got closer, I realized the thing was actually two things, one of them galloping, the other flapping.

Destiny and Thomas!

I ran out of the booth, opening my arms. Destiny flew straight into them, nearly knocking me over. She was honking frantically and her feathers were all ruffled. Thomas halted a few feet away, tossing his head and stomping the grass.

My heart was pounding like horse hooves, too. "Something must have happened at the farm!" I yelled.

Thomas snorted and lowered his neck. I grabbed

his mane and pulled myself onto his back. Destiny settled in front of me.

"Rain! Pip! Get Aunt Doris!" I shouted. "Tell her to meet me at Chuckling Goose!"

I let Thomas choose our route. At the edge of town, he picked his way carefully through the woods, weaving around trees and crossing over a little brook. But once we got to the open meadow, he thundered across it. He didn't stop until we'd reached the farmyard.

I gave him a quick kiss on the neck and slid off. The moment I put Destiny on the ground, she headed to the potager, honking for me to follow. My little goose was braver than brave. I tried to be, too.

Still, I was unprepared for what I found in the garden. Aunt Esperanza was sprawled out in the strawberry patch. La Blanca was standing guard, making small worried honks. I almost didn't recognize my grandie. From the first day I'd met her, she'd been formidable. But now her eyes were closed and her arms were flung out as if she'd been surprised. Her thin white hair was slipping out of its little bun. And her cone hat was gone.

"Grandie!" I cried, dropping down beside her. Gently, I lifted her head into my lap. With two fingertips I felt her throat. There was a pulse, which meant she was alive, but she didn't open her eyes. I wondered if the heat had been too much for her—if that was the reason she wasn't wearing her cone hat. I wanted to get her some water, but I was afraid to leave her.

"I shouldn't have gone to the fair." Two tears dripped down my cheeks and plopped onto hers. Her lips moved. I put my ear closer to her mouth so I could hear.

"Pitchy?" she murmured. Her voice was garbled and throaty, but I knew she was saying my name.

"Yes! Yes, it's me!"

"Guh."

I think she was trying to say "good." I had to get her inside, out of the heat, but I needed help.

Fortunately, it wasn't long before I saw a flash of light. Or maybe you'd call it a twinkle. At first I thought the heat was affecting me, too. But in another moment, I saw a faint outline of a person. Quickly it grew brighter and steadier—and Aunt Doris appeared.

"The others are on the way," she said. "Let's get Espy inside."

CHAPTER THIRTY-SEVEN
Ye olde Doctor's orders

Winnie's mom, Dr. Winston, came to examine Grandie. She'd been a Goose Girl long before she went to medical school. Now she took care of all the residents of Chuckling Goose.

After promising not to make a peep, Winnie and I were allowed to stay in a corner of the small, neat room while Dr. Winston examined Espy. "She's very warm. We'll need to cool her down," she told us. "Winnie, please find a fan. Wyatt should be able to help you with that. And Pixie, please bring a pitcher of cool water and ice chips."

Out in the hallway, Winnie gave me a quick hug. "Once I told you that trouble will always find its way," she whispered, "but here's the other thing about trouble—it's never as strong as kindness."

"Er, okay. Thanks." I hugged her back and headed downstairs. *Kindness is stronger than trouble?* I wondered. What could that mean?

Dr. Winston was holding Espy's wrist when Winnie and I returned with the things she'd asked for.

"Her pulse is slow," she said. "It should improve when we get her cooled down. But she's also got a bump on her head and some black-and-blue marks on her arms and neck, as though someone grabbed her."

Winnie gasped. "But who would do that to her, Mom?"

"I—I think whoever it was also took her hat," I said before Dr. Winston could reply.

"It was stolen?" Dr. Winston looked shocked.

All of a sudden it was hard for me to speak. Grandie had loved that hat so much. Seeing her without it was awful. "She wasn't wearing it when I found her," I whispered.

"I can't imagine who would want it," said Winnie. *But I could.*

"Let's wait until she's strong enough to tell us herself," Dr. Winston murmured, placing a cool, wet cloth across Grandie's forehead. "Please freshen this every twenty minutes for the next two hours. You can also press an ice chip against her lips to moisten them."

"Okay, Mom," said Winnie. I could tell she was used to being her mother's assistant.

"Good." Dr. Winston placed a hand on my shoulder. "Pixie, come with me for a moment."

Out in the hall, she spoke in a whisper. "I know you're worried about the hat, honey, but Espy should improve in a few days. When she does, we can find out what happened and try to get it back."

"It belonged to Mother Goose," I said. "Do you think it had special powers?"

Dr. Winston raised her eyes as if the answer were floating somewhere above her. "I don't know about powers, but that hat has a long history. To Espy it was almost sacred."

I swallowed. "What if she can't get better without it?"

Dr. Winston took my hand. "But she will. Espy's

been waiting a long time for you. She's not going anywhere." She gave me a big, encouraging smile. "I'm going to talk to the Aunts before I leave. I'll be back to check on her tomorrow."

Before I went back to my grandmother's room, I let myself cry a little. I was ashamed of all the mean things I'd thought about her since I'd arrived at Chuckling Goose. And there was something else. Even after I knew that hat had belonged to Mother Goose, I'd made fun of it. With all my heart, I wished I could take back my words.

At dinner we drooped around the table like flowers in need of water. Without Grandie to boss us around, everyone seemed to be distracted.

"Attention please, kiddos," said Aunt Doris, emphasizing her words with a loud gum crack. "While Aunt Esperanza is recovering, we're going to have to work harder than ever. We've got to keep things going or she'll be furious at us."

We Goose Girls sat up taller. Gray, River, and Wyatt elbowed each other into doing the same. Aunt Fancy lifted her sweet, fluffy head. Aunt Bernie adjusted her eyeglasses.

"Espy did ten times as much work as anyone else

around here," Aunt Doris continued. "In addition to the wishing cakes, you apprentices will have to help with the everyday cakes. That's how we earn our dough." She chuckled at her own joke. "Boys, you'll need to continue with your regular chores and help in the kitchen, too."

We all gaped at Aunt Doris.

"But we've never had boys in the kitchen!" protested Aunt Bernie.

"What would Esperanza say?" Aunt Fancy gasped, putting a hand over her heart.

"Nobody's a better helper than Gray!" I burst out. "He's smart, careful, and he can keep a secret."

"River always helps in the kitchen at home," Rain added.

Pip grinned at her brother. "I'll be in charge of teaching Wyatt."

"No-o-o-o!" Wyatt grabbed his head with both hands, making everyone laugh.

"I think Espy would say it's a good idea," declared Aunt Doris. "Chuckling Goose Farm is going modern!"

After dinner the Aunts sat with Grandie. I tried to visit, but they shooed me away. "You don't need to worry, Pixie," Aunt Fancy said kindly. "We're taking good care of her."

"*Please.* I'll just stand quietly in the corner," I whispered.

"You've had a rough day, kiddo," said Aunt Doris. "You should turn in early." She put a hand on my shoulder and escorted me out of the room.

But in the middle of the night, I woke up with a terrible need to check on my great-great-great-grandma. Every step creaked as I made my way down to the second floor. I was certain one of the Aunts was going to burst out of her room and catch me, but all was quiet. Grandie's door was ajar, so I tiptoed inside her room and sat beside her bed. The moon cast a pale light on her face. It looked old and wrinkly, yet beautiful. Although her eyes were still closed, I told her what I needed to say.

"Grandmother, it's me, Pixie," I murmured, leaning close to her ear. "You haven't met the rest of my family yet, so I thought I'd tell you about them now. My mom, Dana, who's your great-great-granddaughter, is a lot like you. She's a super baker and gardener. I know she'd love your potager. And she's really kind—the ladies at the senior home where she works love her."

I reached out and stroked Espy's hand with my fingertips. "You'd love my dad, Phil, too. He can fix anything. He's big—kind of like a giant in a fairy tale—but he'd never hurt a fly. And my baby brother, Sammy, well, he's always a bit sticky. But he loves everyone, and everyone loves him. The thing is, my family is missing a grandmother. We need you and I think you need us. I even wrote a poem about it."

I stopped and closed my eyes for a moment before I recited:

> "You weren't always nice at first
> Or the most polite
> You didn't tell me thank you
> And you hardly said good night
> At sunrise in the kitchen
> I was perky as a daisy
> Yet you still frowned upon me
> As though I were being lazy
> But you would've been surprised
> If you had seen me inside
> 'Cause I'm ornery and stubborn
> And much too full of pride
> In other words, Grandmother,
> I've always been like you

Argumentative and cranky

With a heart truer than true."

Although I wasn't sure if she'd heard me, I felt better. "One more thing," I whispered. "I'm going to get your hat back very soon."

Her hand scrabbled at the sheet a little. When I took it in mine, it felt as frail as a just-hatched gosling. Her eyes were still closed, but her lips began moving. It was hard to make out her words, but I thought I heard, *"Careful of bear."* Then she was silent again.

"Don't worry, I will," I whispered. But I tiptoed out of her room wondering what she'd meant. Was it possible a bear had knocked Grandie down and eaten her hat?

CHAPTER THIRTY-EIGHT
Ye olde False Friends

"It's awfully hot out for gardening," Aunt Fancy fretted, looking through the kitchen window and fanning herself. She glanced at Rain, who was cutting green apples into slices, while I was preparing peanut butter sandwiches.

"I like hot weather," replied Rain. "I dream about it all winter long."

"Besides, it will only be worse later on," I added. "That's why we have to water and weed the potager now. I don't want it to be a mess when Aunt Espy sees it again." I bit my lip, wondering when that would be. Although a week had gone by since she had been injured, Grandie didn't seem to be getting better.

Aunt Fancy's bracelets jingled as she patted my shoulder. "At least eat lunch inside, so you don't get too overheated."

"Don't worry, we'll picnic under a tree," said Pip, pouring lemonade into a thermos. "Summer's passing so fast, we don't want to miss it."

Aunt Fancy nodded. "I liked summer, too, when I was a girl. I think I've forgotten how to enjoy it. All right, go ahead."

The Aunts kept a container of old coffee grinds to spread around the roots of the blueberry bushes, which helped to make the soil acidic. Blueberries love acidic soil and water. So we soaked each bush carefully before we moved on to pick cutworms off the tomatoes. Yuck! With the strawberries, weeds were the problem. If they weren't pulled out, they tried to steal the nutrients the strawberry plants needed.

"You sure know a lot about gardening," said Pip after we'd moved under a leafy maple to have lunch.

"When Aunt Esperanza gardens, she's garrulous,"

I said, grinning at the thought. "I guess I like it. My mom gets chatty when she's gardening, too."

"*Chatty* isn't a word I'd ever use to describe Old Coney," said Rain.

"Yes, she's usually the quiet type, like you, Rainey," Pip teased.

I didn't like hearing Grandie called names anymore, but I wasn't ready to let the others know she was my great-great-great-grandmother. So I ignored the nickname and said, "Actually, Aunt Espy told me something last night."

Pip stopped eating and stared at me. "She did? Why didn't you say so before?"

"Her voice was so weak, it was hard to understand," I said. "It sounded like *careful of bear.*"

"Maybe she was dreaming of bears," said Rain. "Did she seem afraid?"

"I wouldn't say afraid, but she reached for my hand as though she were worried. I'm pretty sure she knew I was there."

"Well, I haven't noticed any bear tracks or bear scat around here," said Rain.

I smiled in spite of my worries. Sometimes I forgot how much Rain knew about animals. "I've been thinking about those three Precious girls we met at the fair—" The sound of a vehicle on our usually deserted road interrupted me. We all turned to see who it was.

"Garrie!" exclaimed Pip. "What's she doing here?"

"Probably she heard that Aunt Espy got hurt and wants to see how she is," I said. "They argue a lot, but I think they like each other." I stood up and scattered my crumbs for the birds.

Aunt Fancy had been right; it was too hot to eat. After we packed up, Pip and Rain went back to help frost the everyday cakes and I headed for the barnyard to find La Blanca. Yesterday, while Dr. Winston was checking on Grandie, I'd asked if she thought a visit from La Blanca might help. I thought hearing her beloved goose honk or feeling her soft feathers would remind Grandie that La Blanca needed her. To my surprise, Dr. Winston had agreed it might be a good idea.

Since Destiny and La Blanca were practically inseparable, I let them both into the house, shooing them upstairs without letting them stop to nibble the carpet runner. Although Grandie had only mumbled a few garbled words since she'd been injured, I was eager to see if Garrie had gotten her to talk, or even to argue. But it was just wishful thinking. The only voice that drifted down the staircase was Garrie's.

"If only you weren't so stubborn, Espy . . . believe me, I had no choice."

Suddenly La Blanca honked like a bicycle horn at an oncoming train. Before I could stop her, she flapped up to the second floor with Destiny close behind. The two of them disappeared into Grandie's room. I raced up the rest of the stairs to the sounds of Garrie shrieking.

When I got to the doorway, I could hardly believe what I saw. Like a lion tamer, Garrie was using a chair to keep La Blanca from biting her. The big goose was doing her best to dart past the chair and attack Garrie. And Destiny was rushing around in circles, nipping at Garrie's ankles.

"La Blanca, stop!" I yelped. "Des! Leave her alone."

Blankie paid no attention to me. She flapped up and nipped Garrie on the ear.

"Ouch!" Garrie shouted, kicking at La Blanca.

"Don't you dare hurt her!" I yelled. I was a little surprised to be on La Blanca's side. But geese were like dogs. They seemed to know who to like or dislike.

Waving my arms and scolding, I managed to drive both geese into Espy's closet. Quickly I closed the door.

"Those blasted birds were more respectful when I was an apprentice here," said Garrie, holding her ear.

"La Blanca's been very upset about Aunt Espy," I said.

"Well, so am I," snapped Garrie. She slid the chair next to Grandie's bed and sat down.

"Can I ask you something?" I didn't wait for her answer. "I heard you tell Aunt Espy you had no choice. What did you mean?"

For a second Garrie's small, sharp eyes rolled up under her lids. Creepy! I backed up against the closet in case I needed help from the geese.

"Oh, it's so awful, I don't know if I should tell you," she cried. "You're just a kid."

"Th—that's okay. You told the aunts, right?"

Garrie was crying now. "No! I'm too ashamed. My poor old friend tried to help me and now look at her."

We both gazed at Grandie. In spite of all the noise, her eyes were still closed and she hadn't moved a muscle.

"I just don't know where to turn for help, Pixie dear," Garrie sniffled.

My ears pricked up—*she knew my real name.* "That's okay, you can tell me." I forced myself to smile.

Garrie blotted at her eyes with a tissue. "It was the

only way I could survive. The store wasn't making enough money anymore."

"What *way?*" I asked. I could tell her tears were fake.

"Not long ago, a woman clinked into the store to buy flour. . . . "

"Clinked?"

"Clinked, clanked, clunked, whatever! She was noisy!" Garrie barked.

"Okay, sorry," I said. "But what did she look like?"

Garrie's eyes rolled back in her head again. "I couldn't tell. She was wearing a long cape with a deep hood that hid most of her face. Do you want to hear more or not?"

Now I was positive I didn't want to know. But I nodded anyway.

"Up at the front counter, I keep three covered stands with everyday cakes that I sell by the slice. That clinking woman couldn't stop eyeing them, and since she was new, I let her try a slice free of charge. She said the only cake she'd ever had that was as good had been made by Goose Ladies. Well, I couldn't help it. I told her I used to be one."

Garrie peered at me as if she was daring me to say something. Somehow I kept my mouth shut and my face blank as a new sheet of paper.

"The old clinker asked if I'd ever heard of a wishing cake," Garrie continued, "and I told her I actually knew how to bake one." She smirked. "Maybe I exaggerated a little."

"Wh-what happened?"

"She ordered one. I made her pay in advance, and charged her a lot, too." Garrie winked.

"Did you? Make a wishing cake, I mean?"

"I tried. But I never was any good at baking those wishing cakes. I guess the clinker's wish didn't come true, because the next day she stomped into my store so furious, one of her ears fell off. I had to glue it back on for her."

Holy goose! I began shaking so hard, I was afraid Garrie could hear my teeth clinking. "What did she do?"

"She said I'd better get her a real wishing cake from dear old Esperanza."

"But Aunt Espy would never sell a wishing cake," I gasped. "Especially not to Raveneece."

Garrie smiled. "That's right, you little fox. *Raveneece Greed.* I believe you already know her."

I stared at her. Not even the word *yes* would come out of my mouth.

"Well, you're right about Espy." Garrie shook her head sadly. It was weird how fast she went from glad to mad to sad. "Although I begged and pleaded, she refused to give me one single cake. Not even when I told her Raveneece had sent her nieces to my store."

"I think I met them," I managed to croak.

"In a single afternoon, those three girls ate every crumb of the everyday cakes I'd ordered for the entire week. There was nothing left to sell. But when I complained to Raveneece, she said I'd better cooperate or she'd send them into my store every day until I was out of business." Garrie stared at me with her strange, rolling eyes. "Now do you see why I had no choice?"

I swallowed. "No choice?"

"I had to steal that big, ugly cone hat, of course! Raveneece said she'd hold it for ransom until Espy changed her mind about the wishing cake."

"So you're the one who took it!" I gasped.

Garrie put a hand over her heart. "I never meant to hurt my old friend. I came back to the farm to give her one more chance. All she had to do was bake me a single, measly cake and Raveneece would never bother either of us again. But Espy wouldn't do it.

She said Raveneece would never be satisfied with one. Then she turned and walked away, like she'd already forgotten about me. I couldn't help it—I got so mad, I grabbed her shoulder. That's when La Blanca came after me."

"Geese have good instincts," I muttered.

"I kicked at that goose like she was a big fat soccer ball," she hissed. "But pigheaded Espy tried to protect her and *oops,* I kicked her instead. She went down so hard, it sounded as if her head cracked. Oh, my poor old friend!" Garrie put her hands over her face. I was pretty sure her tears were phony.

"What happened to the hat?" I asked, fighting to stay calm.

"I brought it to Raveneece, of course."

"But Espy needs it!" I shouted. "It's precious to her, to all of us."

In an instant Garrie shot up out of the chair and loomed over me. "Be reasonable and I might be able to get it back. All you have to do is bake me a wishing cake. None of your Goosey friends need to know. You can just slip it in with my regular order, as if it's an everyday cake.

"You want me to be a liar and thief, like you? Now I know why you couldn't be a Goose Lady!" I reached for the closet doorknob. "Leave, before I let the geese out."

Garrie held up her hands and backed out of the room. "It's for Espy's own good. You'll be sorry you didn't listen, brat."

"GET OUT!" I cracked open the closet door.

HONK!

Garrie fled.

CHAPTER THIRTY-NINE
Ye olde False confession

With Destiny and La Blanca behind me, I ran to the barn to find Gray.

"What's wrong?" he asked when I burst through the door. His eyebrows met in the middle of his forehead like swords. "It's her again, isn't it?" he whispered. "Raveneece?"

I nodded. "She's got Espy's cone hat, Gray."

He sat down on a bale of hay. "I thought you said she'd been shattered."

"She was, the last time I saw her. But remember

that sweeping sound in the woods I told you about? Aunt Doris said it could have been the Broom of Doom." I closed my eyes and recited:

"If you're cracked to pieces
And there's no way you can mend
The Broom of Doom can help you heal
Though it is not a friend

"It may put you back together
But you won't know your own face
For your eyes and ears and other parts
May not fit back in place."

Gray picked at the hay. "If you're thinking what I *think* you're thinking, it's not a good idea, Pix."

"But I've got to get the hat back! I'm afraid Aunt Espy won't recover without it."

"Tell the Aunts. They can call the police."

"They can't do that. No one knows their secret identity. The people in town think they're ordinary bakers. Plus, the police would think they were a bunch of crazy old ladies."

"I guess but—"

"Please, Gray! Espy needs the hat. We all do. It represents our heritage and our mission."

"Okay, okay, but you can't go alone. I'll help you,"

he said. "You'll freeze her and I'll grab it. Then we'll run!"

"No, Gray, no!" I said. "I'll never freeze anyone again. Seeing a person crack into pieces is sickening. You can't imagine."

"But you can freeze her without shattering her, can't you?"

"I'm not sure anymore. I don't know what I can do. Besides, accidents happen." Two tears squeezed out of my eyes before I could stop them.

"It's okay, we'll think of something else." He scratched his head. "Hey! I know! I have my dad's wolf urine spray."

Good old Gray. That stuff was supposed to be used on camping trips to keep predators away from a tent.

"I don't think it'll work on Raveneece. But I know who can help us."

All through dinner I worked up the courage to talk to the other apprentices. I kept thinking that if only I hadn't kept Raveneece's eye splinter a secret, we would have been prepared for trouble. I was responsible for the danger we were in.

At bedtime, when we were all together, I paced

back and forth while the others put clothes away and chatted. Finally, Perrin sent me an amused, sideways look.

"Is anything wrong, Pixie?"

"Yes, a lot!" I exclaimed, louder than I'd meant to. That got everyone's attention. "I need to tell all of you something, but I don't know how."

"You can tell us anything." Perrin patted her bed. I sat, and the rest of the apprentices gathered around. Being together like that gave me the courage to confess what I knew, and to ask for their help.

I began my story back on the first night, when I'd heard the clinking sound and stepped on Raveneece's eye. I told them how Pip, Rain, and I met the three Preciouses at the fair and what they'd said about their aunt having something we'd be begging for. But when I got to what Garrie had said about kicking Aunt Espy and taking her hat, gentle Perrin exploded. "How could she? Let's go get the hat back right now!"

"Wait, there's more." I swallowed because I hated to tell them what came next. "Garrie took Espy's hat—and she gave it to Raveneece Greed."

"Oh my goose!" exclaimed Nell, falling back on the bed. "But I still don't see why Raveneece would want Espy's hat."

"She thinks she can trade it for a wishing cake," I said. "She wants to wish for the ability to rhyme. She's been scheming to bake her own wishing cakes for years."

"Did you tell the Aunts?" Perrin's forehead was crinkled with worry.

"No! Look at what happened to Aunt Espy! I'm afraid they'll get hurt!" I took a deep breath. "But I do know someone who might be willing to help us—another relative of ours. But first we'll have to find her."

The apprentices waited for me to go on. It was hard, because I hadn't forgotten Grandie's words. *What happens between you and the batter must remain private!* But I also remembered what she'd told me when I'd first arrived at Chuckling Goose. *You have to be able to recognize what's most important.* That was the best advice I'd ever heard.

The thing is, I knew I would sound ridiculous, but sometimes you just have to be ridiculous!

"We're going to talk to Mother Goose," I said.

CHAPTER FORTY
Ye olde Fly in the Batter

The kitchen seemed like a completely different place at night—spooky and maybe dangerous. The yellowy lights of the giant oven were like eyes, and its door was a mouth waiting to be fed. The long-necked nozzle in the sink was a wily serpent about to strike. Even Stumpy's shadow made my dear old spoon into a fat-bellied gremlin.

"I can't believe I'm getting to see this," whispered Wyatt as we gathered ingredients and utensils. "I mean, River, Gray, and I have been helping with the everyday cakes since Aunt Espy got injured. *But wishing cakes*—everything about them has always been kept secret from us."

"I think it started because of an old-timey king," I explained while I measured flour, sugar, and cinnamon into a bowl. "He threatened to put Mother Goose in jail if she didn't bake her wishing cakes only for him. That's why she had to go into hiding." I added two teaspoons of baking powder before I continued the story.

"After that Mother Goose must have felt she could only trust her own family, which was all girls at the time. Her secret kept getting passed down through her daughters and granddaughters. But just because it's always been done that way doesn't mean we can't change. You guys are family, too."

"I'm not," Gray said, looking miserable.

"We're making you official right now," said Wyatt, clapping an arm around Gray's shoulders.

"I agree!" Perrin tapped him on the head with her beautiful mixing spoon. "Welcome to the family, Gray Goose-Westerly!" We all clapped.

Gray turned the pinkest pink. "Thanks," he mumbled.

Although I'd already baked wishing cakes on my

own, I was nervous. What if Mother Goose didn't appear in the bowl? I was certain she'd want to help us get back Aunt Espy's cone hat. After all, it used to be hers. But I didn't know if she'd want to be seen by everyone.

I cracked the eggs carefully. I wanted the batter to be perfect for Mother Goose. After I'd mixed in the butter, the milk, and the vanilla, I took Stumpy off the spoon rack.

"Sorry to wake you, Stump," I murmured, dipping my spoon into the batter.

I put my hand over my heart and got ready to recite. All afternoon I'd been so nervous I hadn't known how to start my rhyme. Finally I'd borrowed an old one—"Pat a Cake, Pat a Cake"—that Mom and I used to say when I was really young. I'd worked on it line by line, until it was different, but still familiar:

> "Batter imp, batter imp
> Call the one
> Who'll grant my wish
> So our battle's won
>
> "Stir it, bake it,
> Mark it with M G

Take back your hat and help us save
Your leg-a-cy!"

I held my breath as I hoped for something to happen. It took longer than usual, but the batter imp finally appeared. First the flat lines for eyes. Then the dimpled cheeks and the curvy little mouth.

"*Too wate! Come back tomowwo,*" whined the imp.

"I'm sorry, but this is an emergency," I said in a soothing voice. "Can you please get Mother Goose?"

"*Need a funny wyme!*"

"But I'm not feeling very funny."

"*Make funny!*" the imp insisted.

The truth was, I had a funny rhyme already prepared, because I knew the imp liked to argue before it gave in. "Well, okay," I said. "Here goes:

"You don't have to worry
If a fly lands in your batter
She's really very clean
And she will not make you fatter
Her little legs will kick until
They break up every lump
And your batter will be perfect
Without a single bump
Then make a wish
That says you hope

The fly has a nice day

Now dry her off, say good-bye

And fly will fly away!"

"Night-night!" With a giggle and a splash, the imp disappeared.

"Your imp is adorable!" cooed Nell.

"It's annoying," grumbled Pip.

"I guess each imp is different," said Perrin, being what my mom would call "diplomatic."

"Shush, everyone. I think Pixie needs quiet for the next part," said Winnie. I sent her a grateful smile.

In my head I chanted, *"Please come, please come,"* staring into the bowl until the batter rippled again and a different face began to appear—crinkly eyes . . . a bumpy nose . . . a smile like half an orange . . . and a pointy hat with a round brim.

"It's her!" squealed Nell.

"Holy goose!" Pip exclaimed.

"Shh," said Winnie quietly. "Be respectful."

"My, how many people I see," murmured Mother Goose's warm voice.

"They're your family, too," I said.

Tiny bubbles rose from the batter. "Really? How glad I am to meet you all! Tell me your names."

We went around in a circle until everyone was introduced. Although I was super happy that Mother Goose was pleased, I was also impatient to get to the important part.

"We're here because we need your help," I said. "Aunt Esperanza's cone hat, the one that was yours, has been stolen. Raveneece Greed is holding it for ransom. She wants a wishing cake, so she can get back her rhyming ability."

"She must never have one!" Mother Goose's mouth became a frown.

"Don't worry, we're not giving it to her!" declared Rain.

"But we need your help," I whispered. "I know you spent much of your life trying to keep your cakes safe from people who were greedy and dishonest. I've been wondering if you have any trick recipes to share. Is there a cake that could help us get back the hat without giving away a wish?"

The batter began to swirl—slowly at first, but then faster and faster. Mother Goose's face vanished, but in the next moment, her voice drifted up out of the bowl:

"The recipes are in my book
But you must choose the one

To help you bake a wishing cake
That gets what you want done

"Oh there's magic in the baking
But if the hat you want to win
You must use your clever noodle
To make Raveneece give in!"

CHAPTER FORTY-ONE
Ye olde Riddling Recipe

While the others cleaned up the kitchen, I asked
Rain and Pip to help me search Grandie's office. We
needed to find the fat cookbook she'd brought to our
first baking lesson. There were enough cookbooks in
her office to fill the Library of Congress. They were
shelved in double rows, one behind the other. Others
were stacked on the floor, the windowsills, the top of
the desk, and under the desk. We looked and looked
but couldn't find the one with Mother Goose's hand-
written recipes in it anywhere.

"You know, if it were mine, I wouldn't keep it where anyone could find it easily," said Pip after a while. "I would've hidden it. I'll bet that's what the sneaky old cone hat did."

"Don't call her that," I said quickly.

Pip looked at me, surprised. "Really? I thought you detested her."

"Not anymore," I said.

I began opening and closing Grandie's private drawers, which made me really uncomfortable. Pip didn't seem to mind. But then, she was used to poking around in other people's things.

Suddenly I realized something. "You know, I haven't seen any nursery rhyme books on these shelves," I said. "Where do you think she keeps those?"

Pip shrugged. "You could check that closet." She pointed to a narrow door in a corner of the room.

I swung it open, expecting to find a baggy sweater and maybe some black rubber gardening boots or a watering can. Instead, the closet was lined with shelves full of nursery rhyme books. There was even a shelf on the inside of the door.

"Look!" I exclaimed in a hushed voice.

For a moment the three of us just stood there and stared as if we'd found a cave full of gold.

The brightly colored book jackets made it easy to spot the one we were searching for. Its old linen cover stuck out like a sore thumb. I grabbed the heavy volume and hugged it.

With Rain and Pip gathered around me, I set the book on the desk and opened it. The paper felt so thin I was worried that even a sneeze could tear a hole in it. There wasn't a table of contents to lead us to the recipe Mother Goose had mentioned. We were going to have to search one page at a time—which could take hours. Even worse, Mother Goose's handwriting looked like spider legs. She used the kind of old-fashioned alphabet that made the letter *s* look like an *f* and the letter *w* look like two *u*'s. The hand-written recipes were really hard to read.

We flipped through the chocolate cakes first: chocolate layer, chocolate pound, devil's food, molten chocolate, chocolate decadence, flourless chocolate, chocolate cheesecake, chocolate fudge, chocolate caramel, chocolate chocolate chip, chocolate pudding, chocolate chili, chocolate ice cream, chocolate peppermint, and chocolate dirt cake. (The dirt was crushed cookies, not dirt-dirt.) We didn't even get to the end of the chocolates before we gave up.

"Maybe there's an index," Rain suggested.

Pip rolled her eyes. "What are we going to look under—*t* for trick cakes?"

I ignored her and turned to the back. But Mother Goose didn't seem to believe in indexes, either. Even the last page was a recipe.

"Let's go back to where we left off." I sighed. "We'll have to keep reading all night."

"Pixie, wait!" Rain pointed to the last recipe. "Look at the name of this one."

"*Reversing Cake*," I said, leaning closer. I read the list of ingredients aloud: "Sugar, salt, flour, egg whites, warm water, orange juice, cream of tartar, and a mirror."

Pip snorted. "A mirror? How do you put a mirror in a cake?"

"Maybe we'd have to break it first," said Rain. "A cake like that could bring a lot of bad luck and crack a lot of teeth."

"You know what Aunt Fancy says, 'Always read a recipe through twice.' Then maybe we'll understand," I said.

The first part of the recipe was the usual, like sifting the flour, sugar, and salt together, beating the egg whites, and combining it all. But the second part was written in rhyming verse and there was nothing ordinary about it at all.

> When the batter's in the bowl
> Over it a mirror hold
> Chant your rhyme into the cake
> Stir it up and let it bake
> Once the batter you reflect
> A wish will have reverse effect
> (Though first there'll be a short delay
> While wisher *thinks* she has her way).

"Whoa! It is a trick cake!" Pip exclaimed. "It makes the opposite of what a person wishes for come true."

"But what do you think the last part means?" asked Rain.

I was wondering about that, too. "It sounds like at first it does grant the wish," I said. "But after a little while, the reverse thing happens."

Rain wrinkled up her freckled nose. "Why can't it work in reverse right away?"

I thought for a moment. "Aunt Doris once told me that when Mother Goose decided she would only give her wishing cakes away randomly, there was trouble," I said. "A lot of greedy people tried to get them. They threatened her with all kinds of harm. She must have invented the reversing cake to fool them. A 'short delay' would give her time to get away before the baddies realized they'd been tricked."

"Smart!" Rain's eyes shone like candle flames.

"Yup." I closed the book and tucked it under my arm. "Let's go show this to the others. We've got to bake a reversing cake *now*."

CHAPTER FORTY-TWO
Ye olde Reversing cake

If someone had peeked through the kitchen window,
they might have thought we were a coven of witches.
Winnie, Nell, Rain, and Pip gathered ingredients and
poured them into a bowl. Barefooted and wearing a
white nightgown, Perrin climbed a stool and held her
little silver mirror above the batter while I stirred and
recited the chant that was written below the recipe.

"Batter, batter, see yourself
Before you're sent to bake
You're wet as soup and runny now

Though soon you'll be a cake

"When the wisher's wish is spoken
I trust you won't obey
But turn the meaning inside out
And send it on its way."

I washed and dried Stumpy, wondering if it were the last time I'd see my mixing spoon. I had to clear a lump in my throat before I asked, "Will someone watch the oven while I go up and change my clothes?"

"Why? Where are you going?" said Nell in her high, shaky voice.

"I'm going to bring this reversing cake to Garrie's store and get back the hat. Gray and Pip are coming with me."

"I'll come too," exclaimed Perrin.

I put my hand on her arm to stop her. "No, Perrin, I've thought this out. Winnie is our best nurse. She needs to stay and take care of Aunt Espy. Rain and River can care for Thomas, the cows, and the geese. Wyatt needs to tend the garden and the farm equipment. And you and Nell have to keep on baking wishing cakes. I have no idea how long we'll be away. You have to keep the Goose Ladies' mission going no matter what."

Perrin twisted her golden hair in her fingers. "But the Aunts can do the baking—Doris, Fancy, and Bernie can manage without me."

I shook my head. "They can't know where we went! They'd follow me!"

"They'll find out anyway, Pixie."

"I know. Pip, Gray, and I are leaving now, so we get a good head start before they wake up." I hugged Perrin. "You've got to keep Chuckling Goose safe until we get back," I whispered. "Please."

Her eyes met mine and she nodded.

"Get whatever you need and meet me on the porch," I told Gray and Pip. "There are a couple of things I have to do."

After I'd pulled on jeans and a shirt, I went to Grandie's room. The moment I entered, I sensed something was different. I didn't even have to use my goose flashlight to see that her eyes were open.

"Hi, Grandmother," I whispered. "How are you feeling?"

She was staring up at the ceiling. I couldn't tell if she'd heard me.

"I wanted to tell you I'm going away for, um, well, I don't know how long. But don't worry, I'll be back." I smiled at her in a reassuring way.

She was breathing hard, as if it were a struggle. When I leaned over to kiss her, I caught the lemony scent of the lotion Winnie used to massage her arms and hands. "Don't worry, the others will take good care of you," I promised. When I stood back up, I saw a tear roll down her cheek.

"I love you," I said, "and I think you love me."

I went to the computer room next. It had been a while since I'd sent an e-mail to Lucy and Alexa. I thought I'd better write in case they didn't hear from me for a really long time.

To: Lucy Chang, Alexa Pinkston
Subject: Baking Camp Can Be Dangerous

I'm off on a delivery
But first I need to share
There are some folks who'd kill for cake
It's giving me a scare!
For cake can be more coveted
Than barrels full of gold
And some friends become enemies
When riches they behold
So keep your fingers crossed

While on this mission I embark
And I'll try to be my bravest
Against danger in the dark.

Love, Pix

My last stop was the barn. As soon as she saw me, Destiny honked and came running on her wide orange feet. "Hello, little cowgirl," I said, scooping her up in my arms. She nestled her head under my neck the way she'd been doing since she'd hatched.

La Blanca stood up and waddled over. I sat on the floor and let her climb into my lap. Snuggling with the two of them was almost too cozy to bear. But soon the sound of a barn owl hooting *Who-WHO, Who-WHO* got me moving again. It was Gray's secret call, letting me know it was time to leave. I gave the geese a last hug and set them on the floor. "You two take care of each other," I whispered.

Back in the quiet kitchen, the cake was waiting in a box on the counter. I suppose it was too hard for the others to say good-bye. But they'd left a pile of good-luck charms on the counter: a sparkly hairpin from Perrin, a pretty handkerchief from Nell, a message on a small white card from Winnie that said, "Kindness is the best weapon," and from Rain, the silky cloud-thread I'd given her when she'd left.

I wrapped it around my finger and tucked the rest in my pocket.

"Good-bye," I whispered.

CHAPTER FORTY-THREE
Ye olde Birthday Party

The moon was an icy gray sliver, but even in the dark Pip led the way through the woods with confidence. We took turns carrying the cake. Amazingly, no one dropped it, even though there were plenty of roots and rocks to trip us. Pip said it was usually a twenty-minute walk between Chuckling Goose Farm and Garrie's, but the night was like an extra obstacle, slowing us down. The truth was, a part of me wished we'd never get there.

The grocery was at the edge of town, the last

building on the last block to be exact, and it was small and old-fashioned. The front window was shuttered for the night, but it reminded me of the kind of place where you could buy drinks, candy, and ice cream in addition to milk, bread, and other staples.

"How are we going to get in?" whispered Gray. "Is there a window in the back we can crawl through?"

Pip smiled and tapped her head with a finger. "I've got the key up here." She rubbed her hands together and began reciting:

> "Lock, please honor my request
> And grant what I ask for
> Kindly allow my friends and I
> To pass inside your door."

Pip nodded at the doorknob. "Go ahead; it's open now," she said to Gray.

He reached out and turned it. "Cool," he said.

"Well, then, what are you waiting for?" asked Pip. She slipped inside before we had time to plan anything. I guess she'd spent so much time at Garrie's she felt comfortable. Maybe too comfortable, I thought.

"Here goes," I whispered. Gray followed me, so close I could feel his breath on my neck.

Inside the store it was as dark as if we'd been

wrapped in a black, velvet blanket.

"Welcome! We've been waiting for you," a voice said. I jumped, even though I knew it belonged to Garrie. "One of you lazy girls turn the lights on for our guests," she snapped.

I heard footsteps and after a moment, the room was flooded with light. I looked around, squinting down narrow aisles of groceries. Just a few feet away stood Garrie. She was wearing Grandie's cone hat. Precious Diamond, Precious Ruby, and Precious Emerald were near the cash register, grinning like evil jack-o'-lanterns.

"Good work, Pip, you got her to come. I wasn't expecting the boy, but he's a bonus." Garrie turned and eyed the Preciouses. "I like a girl who gets things done. You three should try to be more like Pip."

Precious Diamond, Precious Ruby, and Precious Emerald glared at Pip.

"Pip didn't bring us. Gray and I made our own decision to come," I said.

"Why of course she brought you. We've been planning this since the morning before you arrived at Chuckling Goose."

I turned and stared at Pip, but she was looking at the floor.

"You knew about this, Pip?" I exclaimed. "Why didn't you tell us?"

"Because she trusts that I know best!" said Garrie. "I've been taking care of Pip since she was a little Goose Girl, even though the Goose Ladies threw me out. I babysat her every day after school until Doris came to get her. I befriended her, gave her candy, and even let her work for spending money. Now she's helping me." Garrie paused. "I mean, helping me help the Goose Ladies."

Precious Diamond smirked. "Friends help friends, right Pip?"

"You're not her friend," I snapped. "You've pinched her black and blue."

"Shh. It's okay, Pixie," murmured Pip. "Garrie's going to return the hat. She only borrowed it, so she could trade it back for a wishing cake."

"But that's thievery!" I exclaimed. "She kidnapped the hat! And you helped her!"

Pip shook her head violently. "You don't understand! Garrie is going to give the wishing cake to Raveneece, to keep her and her Sinister Sisters from harming the Aunts."

"That's right," said Garrie. "And since you're the most powerful Goose Girl, your wishing cake will be the most dependable, right?" Garrie sent me an ugly smile.

"I can't believe you betrayed us!" I said. "Does Wyatt know? Or did you deceive him, too?"

"No," Pip whispered, "he doesn't know."

"Betrayal?" Garrie snorted. "You've got it all wrong. This cake is about helping. Why, it will help my friend Raveneece get back the rhyming power the Sinister Sisters and their descendants lost so unfairly. I'm even having a little going-away party for Raveneece and her nieces tonight. You Goose kids can help us celebrate."

"We didn't come for a party. We came to trade this cake for Espy's hat." I set the cake box on the counter. "Here it is. Now give us the hat and we'll go."

Garrie clucked her tongue. "I'm afraid you'll have to stay awhile. Your Aunt Raveneece is eager to see you." She crooked a finger at Pip. "Go down to the cellar and get her."

"Yeah, you go, Pip," said Precious Diamond, laughing. "Hurry up or we'll give you another nickel."

Without looking at any of us, Pip walked to the back of the store and disappeared.

Gray and I exchanged a quick glance. Soon we heard the slow step-clink-step-clink of someone climbing stairs. A door creaked open. A bat flew into the room.

"Ahhhhh!" shrieked Precious Emerald.

Precious Diamond pinched her. "Quiet, it's just a birdie," she barked.

"It's Ruby's fault! She was supposed to catch that bat." Precious Emerald turned and pinched Precious Ruby.

Ruby squealed and pinched her back.

A woman in a black jumpsuit and a nest hat walked down an aisle toward them, clinking with every step. One of her hands was on Pip's shoulder. The other was using a broom made from a twisted branch for a cane.

It was Raveneece—sort of. She looked like a broken statue that had been glued back together by a monkey. Some pieces of her face were in the wrong place. Her mouth was crooked, though at least it was above her chin. But her nose was upside down, she had one eye above her eyebrow, and there was an eye patch where the other one should have been.

She peered around the room until she saw me. "Come give your Auntie a hug, brat." She reached out a hand and one of her fingers fell off. Pip scrambled to retrieve it.

"We brought you a wishing cake," I said, frozen in my spot. "We're hoping you'll be willing to trade it for Aunt Esperanza's hat. She really needs it."

"We all need things, brat," said Raveneece. "Garrie needs money to run the store, my greedy nieces need cake to eat, and you need to pay for what you've done to me. Do you think a single cake is enough?"

"I only froze you so I could get away. I never meant to shatter you. I didn't even know it could happen. I was trying to return your key and it accidentally hit your head. I'm really sorry."

"Well, that doesn't matter now." Raveneece waved and another finger fell off. She didn't even seem to notice. "Is that a real wishing cake, brat?"

"Y-e-e-es," I mumbled. I'd never been a very good liar.

Raveneece pointed her broom at Garrie. "*She* tried to fool me with a fake one. I paid her a lot of money for a dud. You wouldn't do that, would you?"

"N-n-n-n-no."

"Well, let's try it and see. Open the box, brat."

"It's a snickerdoodle," I said as I lifted the lid. The cake was still warm, and its cinnamon scent began drifting around the room.

"Oh, yummy!" exclaimed Precious Ruby. "Let's eat!"

"Not before we've lit the candles and I've made my wish." Raveneece turned her one eye to me. "Bring it over here."

"First I want Aunt Esperanza's hat back," I said. "Please."

"Go ahead. Give it to her, Garrie," said Raveneece. "You look stupid in it anyway."

"Oh no," said Garrie. "I've decided to keep it. Maybe I'll be the head of the Goose Ladies now."

"But you promised if I brought the wishing cake, you'd give back Aunt Espy's hat," cried Pip.

"Well, I changed my mind!" snapped Garrie. "And you'd better be quiet or . . . "

"I'm not giving anyone this cake unless I get the hat," I said.

"Give it to her, Garrie," said Raveneece. "I want that cake!"

"So do I," snarled Garrie. "I've decided to keep the cake, too, you cracked old thing."

With the cake still in my arms, I began backing toward the door. "I'll smash this cake and neither of you will get it," I threatened.

"You'll lose everything, Garrie," said Raveneece.

"My precious nieces and I will be permanent residents in your cellar. We like it down there. We'll eat up everything you have and then some."

Garrie turned as purple as a bruise. She scowled and stamped a foot. Then she reached up and jerked the cone hat off her head.

"All right, you old goose poop, you win!" Garrie slammed the cone hat on the counter. "But I want you and your useless nieces out of here tonight. And I never want to see you again!"

"That's not very hospitable of you, Garrie," said Raveneece. "I paid you a lot of money for a cake that didn't work. I'd say you got what you deserve."

"Hurry up and get moving, Pixie, Trixie, or whatever your name is," said Garrie, glaring at me. "Put that cake down next to the hat."

I didn't trust either of them, but I wasn't sure what else to do. I wanted to get Mother Goose's hat back to Grandie as quickly as I could. Carefully I put the cake on the counter and reached for the hat.

"Not so fast!" shouted Raveneece, jabbing her broom at me. "First I've got to test the cake. I'm not getting cheated again."

"I've got candles in here," said Garrie. She opened the cash register and grabbed a box from the compartment where dollar bills should have been. "How many do you need?" Her lips formed an ugly sneer. "I doubt there are enough in here."

Raveneece tried sneering back. Her bottom lip slipped sideways and fell off. "All I need is one," she said.

Garrie stuck a pink candle into the middle of the cake. "All right now. Are you ready to make your wish?"

CHAPTER FORTY-FOUR
Ye olde cracked Wish

"First light my candle! Everything has to be exactly right," said Raveneece. "I'm not taking any chances with my wish. I've waited too long."

"All right, all right, give me a minute. Let me think where I put the matches." Garrie tapped her nails against the register. "Ah! I know." There was a wild grin on her face as she bent down to look beneath the counter.

"Hurry up! I don't have all night," croaked Raveneece.

"Found them," said Garrie. But as she stood up, I caught a flash of silver. It was a big pair of scissors with sharp, shiny blades. "Do you know what this is?" Garrie was looking at me.

"S-s-scissors." My voice was barely a whisper.

"Not just any scissors. It's the Shear of Fear."

"Never heard of it," said Raveneece, snorting. "Now quit your baloney and get me those matches."

But Garrie ignored her. She seemed more interested in me, now. "How about a haircut?" she said, opening and closing the evil-looking blades.

"No—no thanks," I said.

"No?" Garrie put a finger to her lips. "Now let me think. What was I going to do with these?" She looked at the cone hat and cackled. "Oh yes! I was going to trim this. It's much too tall."

"Don't!" exclaimed Pip. "Please!"

Garrie waved the shears at Pip. "Didn't I tell you to shut up?" She opened the blades and turned back to the cone hat.

"No!" I screamed. "N-o-o-o-o!!!"

"How about here?" Garrie held the Shear of Fear over the tip of the hat. "Or further down?"

"Cut that out, Garrie—a deal's a deal!" Raveneece swung the Broom of Doom and struck her on the back.

But Garrie grabbed the broom away from Raveneece. "Oh, you want me to cut this, too?" She clicked the blades and some bits of feather drifted to the floor.

"You fool!" cried Raveneece. "That broom's the only way to put the pieces back together. If the brat shatters any of us, we're done for!" She tried to pull the broom away from Garrie. Even with all her clinking pieces, she was surprisingly strong. For a moment I thought she might win—but Garrie suddenly pushed it backward, catching Raveneece off guard. Raveneece lost her balance and crashed against the wall. More of her pieces fell off.

"Aunt Ravi!" yelped Diamond. While she tried to stick Raveneece's right ear back on her head, Emerald scooped up the left one and Ruby found a tooth.

"Say good-bye to the old cone hat," shouted Garrie triumphantly, aiming the Shear of Fear at it.

Gray grabbed a plastic milk crate near the door and, using it like a shield, edged toward her. "Give it back, you cheater! Even with that hat, you could never be a Goose Lady!"

Garrie swerved and waved the Shear of Fear at him.

"Gray, be careful!" I yelled.

Out of the corner of my eye, I saw Raveneece remove her bird's nest hat. Holding it like a Frisbee, she flicked her wrist and sent it zooming toward Garrie. The scissors flew right out of Garrie's hand and clattered to the floor.

"What are you waiting for, brat?" shouted Raveneece. "Stop her!"

Those were the words I needed to hear. Instantly, my hair sprang out in all directions, my brain crackled like lightning, and when I opened my mouth, my words howled like wind:

"Scissors fail and fighting cease

Let this place return to peace

And for the one who is to blame

A punishment is now fair game

For bringing us such pain and sorrows

Freeze her now till three tomorrows!"

Everyone had been staring at me. But now all eyes were on Garrie. She was motionless, as stiff as a statue in a town square. Her eyes were wide with horror and her mouth was a gaping hole. One hand was still up in the air. I gazed at the Shear of Fear lying on the floor. It looked like my mom's sewing shears.

"Well, who's a fool now, Garrie?" jeered Raveneece.

With a creak and a clink, she turned to me. "We make a good team, brat. If you join me and my precious nieces, we can be richer than you can imagine."

"No thanks." Although I was still scared, I smiled a little. "But you . . . you saved Espy's hat. Why?"

"Garrie cheated me before and she was about to cheat me again!" snapped Raveneece. "That bitter old pill didn't deserve the cone hat."

I scooped Raveneece's nest hat from the floor, where it lay beside the scissors. "Here, can we trade?" I asked, holding it out.

Raveneece focused her eye on me. She didn't reply.

"I, er, have something else for you, too." I slipped her other eye out of my pocket and held it up.

Raveneece cocked her head. "You said you were sorry for shattering me. No one in the family ever apologized to me before. Did you mean it?"

"Yes," I said, knowing it was true. "But I have to tell you something you're not going to like."

"Pix!" Gray whispered. "What are you doing?"

I ignored him. I had to. "Your wishing cake will only work for a little while. Then everything will go back to the way it was before."

"How long is a little while?" she asked.

I shrugged. "Maybe just a few minutes."

"Useless," Raveneece muttered.

"No, it's not, Auntie. We can still eat it!" exclaimed Ruby.

When Raveneece sighed, she sounded like a rattling china cabinet. "Take this hat to Esperanza right now, brat," she said, lifting it up from the counter. "Tell her Raveneece says hello and good-bye. My nieces and I are going back home. After we eat up this cake."

I approached her, wondering whether she and the three Preciouses were about to trick me. But I had to be braver than brave. When I got close enough, Raveneece set the hat on my head like a crown. It almost covered my eyes. "I'm sure you'll grow into it," she croaked.

I held up her eye. "If you lean down, I'll put it in place," I offered.

Raveneece took off her eye patch and bent her creaky self so I could press the eye in line with her other one. At the thought of touching her strange, cracked face, my goosebumps got goosebumps. *Kindness is stronger than trouble,* I reminded myself. Now I understood what it meant. Gently but firmly, I pushed the eye into place.

Wearing Mother Goose's cone hat made me feel

ten feet tall. It also made me feel like my neck was going to be permanently crooked. Like two palace guards, Gray and Pip pulled the door open for me.

"Um, good-bye," I said before we walked out into the night.

"Good-bye, Trixie!" called Precious Ruby and Precious Emerald.

"That's *Pixie,*" Precious Diamond told them.

"That's right, Pixie Piper, Goose Lady Apprentice," I said proudly.

"Get going before I change my mind!" Raveneece barked. The clinking she made as she laughed echoed after us.

CHAPTER FORTY-FIVE
Ye olde Homecoming

Out on the street we kept looking over our shoulders. A few times I actually jumped, thinking I felt Raveneece's cold, not-quite-human fingers on my neck. The woods were only a block away, but it felt like a mile. I squeezed my little goose flashlight on so we could see. Gray was right beside me, but Pip kept her distance. Though I could hear her sniffling, I made myself ignore her. She'd led us into a trap. She deserved to cry.

"Thanks, you were braver than brave," I whispered to Gray.

"Well, you were brave and true," he answered. "But Pix, what's going to happen to Garrie?"

"She'll be frozen for the next three days. Then she'll be able to move like normal again. But it's got to be hard to forget a thing like that. I don't think she's going to bother us anymore."

"I sure hope not," he said. "I'm not sure I can forget about it, either, especially when I close my eyes."

"I know. But the good thing is that we were able to save the hat and ourselves. Sometimes, in the middle of a bad dream, like a dream about what happened with Raveneece last time, I'll remember that. And I'll actually be able to tell myself I'm going to be all right."

Just then we heard a thud. And a moan.

"Pip, is that you?" I called.

"Yeah, I'm okay."

"What happened?" I asked.

"Nothing. Just go on without me," she said in a small voice.

I wondered if this was another trap. My hand shook as I searched the ground with my goose flashlight.

"Over there," I whispered. My trusty little beam found her curled up beside an old tree stump.

"Come on, get up," I said.

"Go away."

"Yeah, let's go, Pix," said Gray.

"I'm not leaving you here, Pip," I declared.

"Why not? I'm a traitor."

For just a second, I hesitated. "I would've said 'disloyal.'"

"I was going to say 'double-crosser,'" grumbled Gray.

"I'm not!" Pip cried. "You just don't understand."

"So tell us," I said.

"Pixie!" Gray tugged at my arm, but I shook him off.

"Wait," I whispered.

After a moment Pip began to speak. "When Garrie told me she was trying to protect the Goose Ladies by getting rid of Raveneece, I believed her. That's why I agreed to help. I didn't know she was planning to keep the hat for herself—or the wishing cake." She lifted her head and met my eyes.

I thought about the spots I'd seen on her arms, the black, blue, and red pinch marks. "I don't get it," I said. "You told me those girls were your friends. If you ask me, those girls were the worst friends anyone ever had."

"All my life I wanted friends," Pip answered. "I

was never allowed to go anywhere after school but Garrie's store. And I couldn't bring anyone to Chuckling Goose. The other kids in my class always had after-school playdates." She swiped at her face with a hand. "When I was little, Wyatt and I played together. But in high school, he began joining all these teams and clubs—basketball, baseball, chess, and science stuff. He'll be going to college next year, and I'll be alone. So I made friends with Diamond, Emerald, and Ruby. But they were only using me."

I sort of knew how she felt. Before I'd learned how to make friends, I used to be friendless at my school, except for Gray, of course. But even then, I wouldn't have hurt my family for all the friends in the world. At least, I hoped not.

"You had no right to give away Aunt Espy's hat or a wishing cake," I told her. "You made some horrible decisions."

"Yeah!" said Gray with a grumble. "You're still a traitor, just not as big as I thought."

"But we won't tell anyone at the farm about you yet," I said. "We want to think about it, right, Gray?"

"*No!* But I will if you want me to," he replied. He'd always been a bigger grudge holder than me.

* * *

When we finally reached the farm, I hesitated. "You go on in," I told Pip. "I'm going to the barn to check on Destiny."

Pip climbed the porch steps with her head hanging low. She didn't look back at us.

Watching her made me sigh.

"What's wrong now?" asked Gray.

"You should think about forgiving her," I whispered. "If you haven't had friends, it's hard to know how to be one. But I think she could learn. Anyway, she did the right thing for the wrong reason. I've done that, too."

"Pixie, you are a complicated person, said Gray, emphasizing it with a loud burp.

"Complicated. You mean like math?" I asked. "Fractions?"

"Yep, you're a fraction."

After I made sure Des and La Blanca were okay, I took the secret staircase to the second floor. With every muscle in my body trembling, I let myself into Grandie's room. She was lying on her back with her eyes closed the way I'd left her. Silently, I removed the big cone hat from my head and laid it down beside her.

"I did it. I got back your hat, Grandmother," I whispered. It was impossible to know if she'd heard me. "I didn't give up hope and I don't want you to, either."

Out of the corner of my eye, I saw her hand move. It seemed to be reaching toward me. When I took it in mine, I felt her give my fingers a tiny squeeze.

"Good night," I whispered. "Please get better." I kissed her hand and set it on the hat. For a moment she caressed it. Then her hand slipped off and settled back on the bed.

On my way out of the room, I bumped into Aunt Doris. The whites of her eyes were glowing scarily and her mouth was stretched in a grim line. My breath caught in my throat.

"Eeek!" I squeaked as she grabbed me.

"Oh, kiddo, I was so worried about you," she murmured, enveloping me in a tight hug.

I tugged her into Grandie's doorway. "Look!" I pointed to the cone hat.

Aunt Doris just shook her head and sighed.

"Am I in trouble?" I asked.

"You bet you are!" she whispered. "But we'll talk about it tomorrow. You should go to bed."

"Wait! I won't be able to sleep unless I ask you something. It's really important."

"Okay, but just *one* something." She held up a finger to show she was serious.

I stood on my tiptoes and whispered it into her ear, just in case someone was listening. Around Chuckling Goose, you never knew.

CHAPTER FORTY-SIX
Ye olde Talent

I was as full of hope as a fresh-baked wishing cake the next morning. I knew it was unlikely—*okay, super unlikely*—that Grandie would be in the kitchen. Still, I'd let myself believe that the return of her cone hat would give her back her strength.

But the lights in the kitchen weren't on yet when I tiptoed in and there was no Grandma Espy in her cone hat, either. It would probably take weeks or months before she got better.

To cheer myself up I sang "Climb Ev'ry Mountain"

while I found the ingredients I needed. I wanted to try out my new breakfast creation, Double Peanut Butter and Jelly Muffins. It was a recipe I'd made up just so I could leave one on Grandie's nightstand. Even with her eyes closed, she might be able to smell her favorites.

I'd just put the first batch in the oven when I thought I heard a honk. "Des?" I called softly. When she didn't appear, I began singing again. But the honking got louder. I was sure someone's goose was attempting a duet with me.

Thump, clank! Thump, clank!

"Geese don't clank," I told myself. Someone was heading toward the kitchen. I raised Stumpy, preparing to defend myself.

La Blanca waddled in, followed by Destiny.

"How'd you two get in here?" I exclaimed. I plucked two raspberries out of a bowl and fed one to each. I was going to have to tell Gray to keep a closer eye on them, even though I was glad to see them.

Then I heard a voice. It was hoarse and wavery, but it was singing, "Climb ev'ry mountain!"

"Grandma Espy!" I cried. She was using a cane to support herself as she thump-clanked into the kitchen. Her head and neck wobbled under the big cone hat.

I ran to get her a chair and waited while she let herself sink into it.

"Something smelled too good to resist," she said.

"I invented a new kind of muffin for you this morning," I said. She interrupted with a thump of her cane.

"I invented something new for you, too," she announced. "I thought of it last night."

La Blanca honked and pulled at the bottom of her purple bathrobe. Grandie waved a hand for me to pick up her goose and set her in Grandie's lap. Even in her fuzzy purple robe and slippers, she looked exactly like a picture book Mother Goose, especially when she began reciting:

"Who's always turning the world on its head?
The girl with a talent for trouble
She can make you so mad that you're seeing red
And your heart swells and pops like a bubble

"Her motives are good, though not oft understood
But we still thank our lucky stars
For a girl brave and true, as ever we knew
And that talented girl is ours."

I could practically feel my freckles glowing. "Did you have a talent for trouble when you were a kid?" I asked.

Grandie's voice was already a little crankier when she answered, "Not as big as yours." She pointed her cane at the oven. "See that smoke? Your muffins are burning!"

CHAPTER FORTY-SEVEN
Ye olde Punishment

While the goose girls went off to write wishing rhymes and the boys went off to collect goose eggs, I remained at the dining table. The Aunts, except for Grandie, who still needed rest, had ordered me to stay put. Even though I'd rescued Mother Goose's cone hat, I was in a heap of trouble for sneaking out of Chuckling Goose at night . . . with a trick wishing cake . . . and going where I shouldn't have gone.

I'd been braver than brave and truer than true. But maybe I'd also been dumber than dumb.

"Didn't you learn anything from your last run-in with Raveneece?" scolded Aunt Bernie. "You're a serial offender, Pixie!"

Aunt Fancy shook a finger stacked with rings at me. "You might have spent the rest of your life underground!"

"I know. But it's not true that I didn't learn anything! When I first got here, Aunt Espy said I needed to learn to recognize what's most important. Well, seeing her get better was the most important thing to me. I thought if I got back her hat, it would help. And I think it did a little."

I looked at each of my Aunt's faces. They didn't look angry anymore, just really frustrated. "I'm not saying I shouldn't be punished," I told them. "I know I broke the rules."

Aunt Doris tapped her red fingernails against the table. "That's part of the problem, kiddo. We tried grounding you, but it didn't work."

"Yes. So we thought we'd ask what you think would be a stiff, but fair, punishment," Aunt Fancy explained.

I'd never been asked to design my own punishment before. It seemed like having a Get Out of Jail Free card.

"Well, you could make me scrub the kitchen floor every day for the rest of the summer. Or you could take away my TV privileges so I couldn't watch *Good News of the Week* anymore. But neither of those are really stiff punishments." I swallowed when I thought about what would really be bad. "The very worst thing would be keeping me away from Destiny, but that would be punishing her, too. She'd be really sad if she couldn't see me. I guess the second worse thing would be taking away my baking privileges and not letting me make wishing cakes anymore."

The Aunts looked at one another with solemn faces. "We'll discuss it and let you know our decision later," said Aunt Bernie finally. "You can go now."

"Okay, thank you," I said. "But can I ask a question first? Have you decided on that thing I asked Aunt Doris about last night?"

"We haven't had time yet, kiddo," replied Aunt Doris. "We'll let you know soon."

On my way down the hall, I passed the wishing room. The door was already closed. I knew the rest of the apprentices were writing their poems. But I wasn't really in the mood for rhyming. Instead, I collected Destiny and La Blanca from the barnyard and brought them to the pond. I was surprised to find

Pip there with her goose. I guess neither of us was ready to get back to ordinary life.

The long grass tickled my legs as I sat down beside her. It was calming just to watch the geese dabble in the water.

"What did the Aunts want?" Pip asked after a while.

"They're deciding my punishment."

She eyed me sideways. "Your punishment? What about mine?"

"I didn't tell on you. I've decided your punishment myself." I bit my bottom lip to keep from grinning.

Pip snorted. "Okay, what?"

"You're coming home with me for the last two weeks of the summer."

She narrowed her eyes. "What kind of punishment is that?"

"Well, you'll have to sleep in a sleeping bag on the floor of my room, which is really tiny. And you'll have to play with my brother."

"Anything else?"

"Yup. You'll have to be my *real* friend, and Gray's. And meet my other friends, too."

"They won't want to be friends with me."

"You'll have to figure out how to get them to like

you. That's why it's a great punishment," I said. "Though the Aunts still have to agree to it. I've already asked Aunt Doris to talk to the others." I looked over my shoulder at the farmhouse. "They're probably deciding your fate right now."

"I don't get it. Why are you being so nice to me?" Pip asked.

I sighed. "I think it's probably because we're alike. You did the wrong thing for the right reason. I have that problem sometimes. Also, because we're cousins, and friends." I hesitated a moment. "Right?"

Pip looked me in the eye and nodded. "Right."

CHAPTER FORTY-EIGHT
Ye olde next Mountain

I guess I should have checked with my parents when
I first thought of the idea. But as usual, I'd gotten
things backward. I'd asked the Aunts for permission
to bring Pip home with me. I'd already invited her.
I'd even talked Gray into thinking it was a decent
idea. But I hadn't checked with my parents. The
truth was, I hadn't called them at all this summer
and I'd hardly written. Which was why I was nervous as I closed myself in Grandie's office the next
morning and lifted the receiver.

The sun was just rising, but I knew my family would be up. We were early risers. We liked having time for breakfast together.

"Awwoh?"

"Sammy? Hi! It's Pixie."

"Peeksie! Hi—hi—hi—hi—hi!"

"Hi, Sammy! Can I talk to Mom or Dad?"

"Hi—hi—hi—hi—hi!"

"Hi, Sammy. Go get Mommy or Daddy."

"Hi—hi—hi—hi—hi!"

I'd nearly given up when I heard Mom say, "Sammy, who are you talking to? Let me have the phone."

"Mom, it's me!"

"Pixie! Is everything okay?"

"Yes, great. I can't believe Sammy is answering the phone now."

Mom laughed. "Only if we don't catch him first."

I imagined her the way she always looked in the morning—messy-haired, barefoot, and moving as gracefully as a cat. It made me feel teary, but in a good way.

"Are you having fun?" she asked.

"Yes. I have so many things to tell you when I get home. But right now I have a question. Would it be okay if I bring someone with me at the end of the summer?"

"Sure. You mean for a weekend?"

"No, um, for two weeks before school starts. Her name's Pip and she lives here at Chuckling Goose. When the kids all go home, she stays here with the Goose Ladies and her brother, Wyatt. But he's busy. And he'll be going away to college soon and I think she's lonely."

"Well . . ."

"Please, Mom. She could stay in a sleeping bag in my room. We'll be helpful—we can babysit. And we're learning to cook!"

"Okay, okay. I'll talk to Dad. I'm pretty sure he'll approve."

"THANKS, MOM!!!"

I couldn't wait to tell Pip. But first I had to make Grandie's breakfast and take it up to her. It was my responsibility every morning. That was the punishment the Aunts had given me for breaking the rules.

Big whoop!

I cooked her a green apple and goat cheese omelet and set a peanut-butter-and-jelly muffin on her bread plate. Out in the potager, I picked a rose and some fresh raspberries. While I was setting her tray, a yawning Gray brought Destiny and La Blanca into the kitchen so I could bring them upstairs to see Grandie, too.

"Did you speak to your parents yet?" Gray asked.

"Yup."

"Is she coming?"

"Yup."

Gray heaved a sigh. "Now Winged Bowl will have *two* girls with a talent for trouble," he said. "It's worse punishment than having to muck out Thomas's stall by myself every day for the rest of the summer."

"You're kidding, right?"

His face cracked a grin. "Yep. I figure at least being home again won't be boring."

We both laughed like it was a big joke. But I had a feeling he was right.

When I got to Grandma Espy's door, I didn't knock. Instead, as I entered with her breakfast, the geese began honking and I began singing: "Climb ev'ry mountain . . ."

To: Lucy Chang, Alexa Pinkston
Subject: What I Learned This Summer

Can a villain be nice?

Can a hero be mean?

Is there a description that fits in between?

Magical powers can make villains weak

They can make children strong

They can make batter speak

But more mighty yet

Are the heart and the mind

They can change cruel to kind

With a story or rhyme

Love,

Pix

P.S. I'm bringing a friend home with me.

I can't wait for you to meet her! See you sooooon!

Recipes for Aspiring Apprentices, from the Goose Ladies

Do you want to be a Goose Kid
With a talent and a mission?
Then why not try these recipes
From Esperanza's kitchen?

Snickerdoodle, Birthday Wish
Are two that you could make
Unless you need a tricky treat
Like the Reversing Cake.

For breakfast try our Biscuits,
But remember not to blink
Or the naughty rolls will fly away
Much quicker than a wink.

And if you want to have some fun,
There's one that's just for play—
A recipe for sparkly snow
To cool a summer's day.

The Goose Ladies' Rules

1. An adult must be present whenever an Apprentice uses the oven or the range top.
2. Line up the ingredients and baking implements before you begin.
3. Read the recipe through twice.
4. Always clean up when you are finished baking.
5. Share and enjoy!

Pixie's Favorite no-Bake Snickerdoodle cupcakes

You say nothing rhymes with *cinnamon*?
Well, how about the *giant grin*
That comes with snickerdoodle cake
These cupcakes are one kind we make

INGREDIENTS FOR THE CUPCAKES

4 tablespoons (½ stick) butter
4 cups miniature marshmallows
4 cups any crunchy, cinnamon-flavored cereal
2 teaspoons ground cinnamon

INGREDIENTS FOR THE FROSTING

3 cups powdered sugar
⅓ cup butter, softened
1 ½ teaspoons vanilla extract
1 to 2 tablespoons milk
1 to 2 teaspoons ground cinnamon

DIRECTIONS FOR THE CUPCAKES

1. Line nine regular-size muffin cups with paper baking cups.

2. Spray an ice-cream scoop with no-stick cooking spray.

3. Put the cereal into a plastic bag. Use your hand to crush the cereal.

4. In a 2-quart saucepan, heat the butter over medium heat until completely melted.

5. Add the marshmallows and keep stirring until all of them are melted. Remove the saucepan from the stove.

6. Stir in the crushed cereal and the cinnamon so that the cereal is evenly coated.

7. With the ice-cream scoop, scoop the mixture into the nine muffin cups.

8. Let the cupcakes cool for about 10 minutes. While they cool, make the frosting.

DIRECTIONS FOR THE FROSTING

1. In a medium bowl, mix the powdered sugar and butter with a spoon, or use an electric mixer on low speed.

2. Stir in the vanilla extract, **1 tablespoon** of the milk, and the cinnamon.

3. Slowly add just enough of the milk you have left to make the frosting smooth and spreadable. (If the frosting is too thick, add a drop more milk. If the frosting is too thin, add a little powdered sugar.) Frost the cupcakes and enjoy!

Nell's Feel-Like-You're-Flying Biscuits

The trick with these is a light touch
You mustn't knead them very much!

INGREDIENTS

2 cups all-purpose flour (not self-rising!)
Several extra tablespoons flour to spread on work surface
2 teaspoons baking powder
1 teaspoon salt
½ teaspoon baking soda
7 tablespoons unsalted butter, cut into thin slices
    and chilled in freezer until hard
¾ cup cold buttermilk
2 more tablespoons buttermilk for brushing biscuit tops
Butter, honey, or jam to serve with biscuits

DIRECTIONS

1. Preheat oven to 425 degrees.

2. Line a baking sheet with parchment paper.

3. Whisk flour, baking powder, salt, and baking soda together *twelve times* in a large bowl.

4. Cut frozen butter into flour mixture with a pastry blender until the mixture looks crumby or bumpy. This will take about 5 minutes. If you don't have a pastry blender, use a fork or the side of a spoon.

5. Use a spoon to make a well or depression in the center of the butter-and-flour mixture.

6. Pour in the ¾ cup buttermilk and stir until just combined. *(Not more!)*

7. Turn dough onto a floured work surface. Using your hands, pat it together into a rectangle. Don't worry if it looks messy. It's supposed to be that way

8. Fold the rectangle in thirds, the way you would fold a sheet of paper to put it into an envelope. Gather any crumbs and flatten back into a rectangle again. Repeat twice more, folding and pressing dough *a total of three times.*

9. Using a rolling pin, roll dough on a floured surface to about ½ inch thick. Cut out 12 biscuits using a round biscuit cutter, or drinking glass, about 2 ½-inches in diameter.

10. Transfer biscuits to the prepared baking sheet. Using your thumb, press an indent into the top of each biscuit. (Thumbprints help the dough to rise up straight!)

11. Brush a little of the 2 tablespoons of buttermilk onto the top of each biscuit.

12. Bake in the preheated oven until browned, about 15 minutes, and remove carefully. Transfer to a plate. Serve with your choice of butter, honey, or jam.

Although these biscuits will be light and flaky, they won't fly out of the oven. But for an extra-special Pixie Party, you can thread a large-eyed needle with kitchen string (made out of cotton!) and poke it through the top of an unbaked biscuit. Tie the ends of the thread in a simple loop and bake. Once your biscuit is out of the oven, attach a helium balloon by its string through the biscuit loop. If the biscuit is light enough, you will have a flying biscuit.

Super-chocolatey Birthday Wishing Cake

If you know someone with a dream
You want to make come true,
Baking them a wishing cake's
The perfect thing to do!

Into the batter you must chant
The most important part:
A rhyme that you've created
With your words and with your heart.

Here's one more thing to close this rhyme:
Baking this cake takes LOTS of time!

INGREDIENTS FOR THE CAKE

1 wishing rhyme that includes the words
   "wish" and "hope"
2 cups sugar
1 ¾ cup unbleached all-purpose flour
1 cup unsweetened cocoa powder
A little extra cocoa powder for dusting pans
2 teaspoons baking soda
1 teaspoon baking powder
¼ teaspoon salt

1 cup freshly brewed coffee or 2 teaspoons instant espresso powder dissolved in 1 cup boiling water, cooled to room temperature *(Note: If someone in your family drinks coffee in the morning, ask him or her to make an extra cup and put it aside for you.)*
1 cup buttermilk at room temperature
½ cup (1 stick) unsalted butter,
    melted and cooled to room temperature
3 large eggs at room temperature
2 teaspoons vanilla extract

INGREDIENTS FOR THE FROSTING

1 pound (4 sticks) unsalted butter at room temperature
1 pound cream cheese at room temperature
2 pounds confectioner's sugar
2 teaspoons vanilla extract
Tube(s) of icing in your choice of color or colors

DIRECTIONS FOR THE CAKE BATTER

1. Preheat the oven to 350 degrees. Position a rack in the center of the oven.

2. Lightly butter three 8-inch round cake pans. Line the bottom of each with parchment paper, butter again and dust with cocoa powder and tap out the excess.

3. In a large bowl, sift or stir together the sugar, flour, 1 cup cocoa powder, baking soda, baking powder, and salt.

4. Add the cooled coffee, buttermilk, butter, eggs, and vanilla extract to the dry ingredients.

5. Over the bowl, chant the wishing rhyme you created.

6. Using a mixer set at low speed, beat for 2 minutes until the batter is smooth.

7. Scrape the batter into the prepared pans. Bake for 25 to 30 minutes until a cake tester or toothpick inserted into each layer comes out clean. Cool the layers in their pans for 10 minutes, then invert them onto racks to cool.

DIRECTIONS FOR THE FROSTING

In a large bowl, use your mixer to cream the butter and cream cheese together on medium speed for 2 to 3 minutes until they soften and combine. On low speed, gradually add the confectioner's sugar and vanilla extract, and then increase the speed and mix for 3 to 4 minutes. Scrape the sides several times during the mixing.

DECORATING THE CAKE

1. Place one layer on a cake plate. Add a generous amount of frosting and spread it on top of the layer.

2. Add the second layer and repeat until all of the layers have been added.

3. Finally, cover the top and sides of the cake in frosting.

4. Use the tube(s) of icing to write the birthday person's name and any message you wish.

Reversing cake

Pretty on the outside,
But the wish thief will pay—
For the thing that she asks
Will fast slip away.

INGREDIENTS FOR THE CAKE

1 tablespoon butter for greasing pan
½ cup unsweetened cocoa powder
1 cup all-purpose flour
1 cup sugar
½ teaspoon baking soda
½ teaspoon salt
6 tablespoons (3/4 stick) butter, very soft
2 tablespoons canola or safflower oil
2 large eggs
1 teaspoon vanilla extract
½ cup cool water
A mirror
The chant (see below)

DIRECTIONS FOR THE CAKE

1. Preheat oven to 325 degrees.

2. Cut the 6 tablespoons of butter into pieces and leave out on the counter to soften. Or you can press the pieces between two sheets of wax paper and use a rolling pin to soften them.

3. Use butter to grease a round or 8 × 8 inch square pan. If you prefer, line the pan with parchment paper.

4. With a fork or spoon, mix flour, sugar, cocoa powder, baking soda, and salt in a large bowl.

5. Add softened butter, eggs, oil, vanilla extract, and 2 tablespoons of the water. With an electric mixer, beat on low speed until ingredients are moist.

6. Turn the mixer to medium speed and beat for a minute. Using a spatula, scrape the batter down the sides. Add the remaining water and beat with mixer for another 30 seconds until the batter is smooth.

7. Now say this chant over the bowl:

When the wisher's wish is spoken,
I hope you won't obey
But turn the meaning inside out
And send it on its way!

8. Scrape the batter into the pan and bake for 30 minutes. Poke a toothpick into the center. If it comes out clean, the cake is done.

9. Cool in pan for 10 minutes. Then turn cake out onto a rack or plate to cool completely (at least half an hour).

FROSTINGS

You will be making two frostings for your Reversing Cake—one chocolate and one vanilla.

INGREDIENTS FOR BOTH FROSTINGS

A mirror
6 cups powdered sugar (3 cups for each frosting)

²/₃ cup butter or margarine, softened
3 ½ teaspoons vanilla extract
6 tablespoons milk
3 ounces unsweetened baking chocolate,
   melted and cooled
2 tubes of icing, 1 chocolate and 1 vanilla

DIRECTIONS FOR VANILLA FROSTING

1. In medium bowl, mix powdered sugar and butter/
margarine with spoon or electric mixer on low speed.

2. Stir in vanilla extract and 1 tablespoon of the milk.

3. Gradually pour in the second tablespoon of milk, a few
drops at a time. If frosting seems too thick, add up to 1
more tablespoon.

4. Beat with mixer until smooth.

DIRECTIONS FOR CHOCOLATE FROSTING

1. In medium bowl, mix powdered sugar and butter/
margarine with spoon or electric mixer on low speed. Stir
in vanilla extract and chocolate.

2. Gradually add 2 to 3 tablespoons of the milk and stir. If
frosting seems too thick, add up to one more tablespoon.
Beat with mixer until smooth.

HOW TO FROST A REVERSING CAKE

Using a frosting spatula or butter knife, cover half of the
cake with chocolate icing and half with vanilla.

Now you will write the word REVERSING on the cake—
from left to right *and* backward: ƆNISЯƎVƎЯ

Be sure to use the vanilla icing tube on the chocolate side, and the chocolate icing tube on the vanilla side.

Hold the mirror over the cake and you will see the word REVERSING.

Everyday Snow

When the grass underneath is grilling your feet
And the sun's shooting rays from the skies,
Not even a gallon of lemonade
Will keep the sweat out of your eyes,
When it seems as if only winter will help
But there's months and months to go,
Then it's time to conceive the perfect reprieve
By making summer snow!

INGREDIENTS

2 ½ cups baking soda
½ cup white hair conditioner (lotion)

DIRECTIONS

Measure the baking soda into a bowl. Add the hair
conditioner and mix with a spoon until blended.

Knead the mixture with your hands until it sticks together
so that it can be rolled into a snowball or molded into a
mini snowperson.

THIS SNOW IS ONLY FOR PLAY. DO NOT EAT!